ELECTRICITY

This is an IndieMosh book

brought to you by MoshPit Publishing
an imprint of Mosher's Business Support Pty Ltd

PO Box 4363
Penrith NSW 2750

indiemosh.com.au

A catalogue record for this work is available from the National Library of Australia

NATIONAL LIBRARY OF AUSTRALIA

https://www.nla.gov.au/collections

Title:	Electricity
Author:	Tunks, Wayne (1975–)
ISBNs:	9781922812124 (paperback)
	9781922812131 (ebook – epub)
	9781922812148 (ebook – Kindle)
Subjects:	YOUNG ADULT FICTION/Fantasy/General; Science Fiction/General; Superheroes

Cover concept by Wayne Tunks at tunks.com.au

Cover design and layout by Ally Mosher at allymosher.com

Cover images used under licence from Envato Elements.

ELECTRICITY

Wayne Tunks

Also by Wayne Tunks:

Normal or Nothing Like It

To my students past and present
who always inspire me

CHAPTER ONE:
KYLE

Screaming. There was always screaming. His mother was crying — he hated that sound more than anything.

She was screaming, 'Sorry'.

That's what angered Kyle the most. His mother had nothing to be sorry for, except for not walking out the door a hundred times. Kyle had never really known what hate felt like, that was until his stepfather came along. Now it seemed an all-encompassing emotion.

Shane seemed nice at first. Kyle's dad had been gone so long, and he wanted his mother to be happy. And, at first, she was.

He took them places, was teaching Kyle to drive, even though he was too young to have a license. Then things slowly changed. Shane became complacent and more demanding. There were also the fits of rage and jealousy. If Kyle's mum came home a few minutes late from work, Shane accused her of infidelity.

Then there was the first time Shane hit Kyle's mum. Kyle remembered it so clearly.

It was a Friday and it had just gone 9.30pm. Kyle and his mum were having a nice evening with pizza and a movie.

Kyle's mum laughed during the film; he only noticed because it was the first time he'd heard her laugh in ages.

All that was broken when Shane burst through the door with the smell of stale beer as his aftershave. He was screaming, his words mostly incoherent. It was something about there being no dinner for him. Kyle didn't think he'd ever heard so many swear words screamed in such a small amount of time. Kyle's mum rose and tried to calm him, only angering him further, and before long the boundary had been crossed and Kyle's mum had been punched.

Kyle immediately rose to her defence, putting on all the bravado he could through his sheer terror. Soon he was also lying on the floor, blood pouring from his nose. He'd reached for the phone; the police only three digits away. After only two zeroes it was his mother who'd hung up the phone. Kyle protested, but he knew he couldn't go against his mother.

So, the silence continued, and with silence came violence.

Tears streamed down Kyle's face as he heard his mother scream again. Every part of him wanted Shane gone, whether that was in a body bag or not, it didn't matter. When Shane wasn't around, he pleaded with his mother to leave, but it always fell on deaf ears. Kyle felt like a failure. A failure as a son and as the original man of the house. He wanted to help his mother, but he felt tied to his chair with fear.

Kyle lacked confidence, ever since his father left. He was only seven at the time, but the memory felt like yesterday.

Kyle's football team had just played in a big football grand final. They were favourites to win, but things had fallen apart on the day, and the team had suffered a crushing defeat — their first of the season. That night, his parents had argued until all hours; Kyle remembered watching the walls of his room shake.

The next morning, his father was gone, for good, and

Kyle felt responsible. He knew his parents had married young. He knew they had their problems, and he knew they loved to argue; but a part of him had always wondered that if he had won the game, would his father have stayed?

Kyle was a good-looking boy; every girl at school knew it. It was his lack of confidence that stopped most of them talking to him. Even with his sandy blonde hair, golden tanned skin and piercing blue eyes, he never knew how to talk to girls. Most of the guys forgot he was in class, and the girls just wished he would talk, so they could at least see if they were interested. He would instead spend lunch holed up in the music room, strumming chords on his acoustic guitar.

He had always been such an outsider — he knew nothing else.

As Kyle sat at his desk in his room, tears streaming, he wanted to be free. Free from his fear, free from Shane, and free from this life that seemed to keep him trapped. His homework had sat in front of him for hours; he barely attempted a question. Next to his textbook lay a newspaper. The front page celebrated the story of a girl in Sydney who had saved her family in a late-night burglary by hitting the thief on the head with a fry pan. She smiled awkwardly on the paper's cover, and Kyle wished he knew her, or at least knew her strength.

He heard his mother scream again, a piercing scream. It was followed by a big and scary-sounding thud. That was it. He could no longer sit idly by while his mother was hurt. Fear would no longer paralyse him. Now was the time, he had to save his mother.

He stood, mustering all the courage he could. As he stood, his hand leant on the photo of the Sydney girl, Parker. That's when it happened.

An amazing blue bolt of electricity radiated between Kyle and the photo of Parker. It warmed Kyle's skin, and instead of being shocked, he felt a sense of comfort from the sight of this strange blue light.

Suddenly, the light shot out of the room, disappearing into the house. There was a loud explosion, and then the sound of Shane screaming in pain.

Without hesitation, Kyle sprinted through the house, knocking over the vase in the hallway. It shattered everywhere. He didn't stop to pick it up, he needed to know what had happened to his mother, where that beautiful bolt of blue had come from, and where it had gone.

As he pushed open the door to his mother's room, he noticed a scorch mark on the door and the subtle aroma of wood cinders. Inside the room, all he could see was carnage. His mother's bed lay in pieces on the floor; the feathers from the pillows flying lazily through the air. Small fires were slowly dissipating around the room, and both Shane and Kyle's mum lay on the floor.

Kyle rushed straight to his mother's side. Her nose was bloody, her eye was raw, but she looked relatively fine, albeit stunned.

'What happened?' whispered Kyle's mum with a laboured voice.

'I don't know,' was Kyle's honest response.

Everything seemed so remarkable and unreal.

CHAPTER TWO:
PARKER

Parker felt like every pair of eyes watched her as she walked through the front gate of school. She had hated the daily routine of walking through the crowd of students ignoring her, but now she was being watched, it seemed unbearable. There were whispers, there were stares, and there were pointed fingers. When Parker stared back at someone, they would nervously smile or turn away. Public recognition — Parker's ultimate hell.

Parker resented the loner tag she had always been laboured with. She wasn't alone, her best friend Beau was practically stapled to her side. And wherever Parker and Beau went, Mel was sure to be a step behind. They were an unstoppable trio. Why was anyone else needed?

Parker kept her head down and let Beau be her eyes. He would fill her in on who was watching and what he thought they were saying. Beau reported that even the teachers were staring. Kids she didn't even think knew she existed; they all suddenly knew her because of that dreaded newspaper article. She was so angry she'd let her parents convince her to take part in it.

Parker had managed to avoid talking to anyone and finally reached her locker. She wondered if she could just crawl in and hide there until 3pm. As she opened her locker, a fry pan fell to the floor — the metallic sound echoing through the hallway.

Everyone around her laughed, except Beau and Mel. Hell was a hallway in Parker's school.

Parker had only recently turned fifteen and was not a fan when she looked in the mirror. She had started getting pimples, and the make up her mother bought her seemed to make them worse. Her hair was a mousey brown and seemed to get frizzy from the smallest amount of humidity. Parker longed to be out of the isolation of her crowded suburban town; she wanted to start the life she knew she was destined to have. And that could never start here.

She wanted to go to university where she could discuss politics and literature and not be called a dork for her interest in current events and old literature. Parker knew it was going to be a few long years until she was able to escape to uni. Her mother told her the boys didn't understand her beauty, that she would come into her beauty at uni. Parker wanted to ask if that meant her mum thought she was ugly, and she wanted to tell her there were more important things in life than having a boy think you're pretty.

Instead, she chose to not prolong the already painful conversation.

Parker knew she wasn't ugly; she just didn't put a lot of effort into her appearance. She was of average height and size and hated pretty things. She knew the pretty things hated her right back.

The incident with the fry pan had thrust her centre stage, a place she never wanted or craved. She didn't even know what the big deal was. She did what anyone would do. She protected her family with a shot her dad joked could see her win gold at the Olympics.

It was late that 'fateful' night. Her family were asleep, and she was tossing and turning in bed — biology tests always kept her awake. She heard a noise in the kitchen, and she thought it was her little brother again. Alistair had serious food issues. He was only twelve but was already the biggest in his grade. Their parents placed him on a killer diet, which left him scouring the kitchen late at night, hoping to raid the fridge for anything with flavour.

Parker had been ready to scare the hell out of Alistair, expecting to catch him in the partial light of the fridge door with a chicken drumstick in his hand and a guilty look on his face. Instead, through the half-moonlight cascading in the kitchen window, she saw a stranger in her kitchen shoving her mother's best silver quietly into a backpack.

With her heart jumping into her throat, she quickly ducked behind the kitchen bench. She had no idea who this man was and what he wanted. *Is he armed? Is he alone? Is he some kind of murderer or rapist?* She could only see his feet — his dirty, big black boot-wearing feet. And they were turning towards her.

She had never been more scared, and she was worried that this was it. All her plans for the future would be gone in a heartbeat. He was getting closer. *Does he know I'm here?* The direction of his footsteps seemed to say he did. And even if he didn't, any second now he would see her huddled in sheer terror.

It was then she saw that infamous fry pan. That heavy old fry pan that her mum had refused to throw away. It had been a wedding present but had always been unused and impractical, and her mum had refused to part with it. 'If it was good enough to give, it's good enough to keep,' her mother would say. And for the first time ever, Parker was happy about that.

She grabbed the heavy handle with all her might. She didn't feel its weight — adrenaline coursing through her veins. Like a gladiator wielding a sword, Parker gripped the fry pan, stood, and in one quick movement swung and struck the intruder. *Whack!* She connected with his nose, and he fell backwards, breaking one of her mother's brand-new kitchen chairs.

He was sprawled on the floor, groaning, almost unconscious with blood pouring from his nose. Then Parker did what any self-respecting girl being attacked would do, she jumped on top of him, continuing to beat him with the fry pan. He was so weak he could barely fight back and was soon unconscious.

Next, Parker's parents were turning on the lights and standing in their pyjamas with mouths open. Soon her mother was calling the police while holding her daughter tightly, and her father had the biggest kitchen knife he could find and was ready to threaten the intruder if he woke up. But Parker had well and truly subdued the man. Her mother was already calling Parker, 'her saviour'.

It was in that moment when Parker's blood pressure finally subsided and normality started to sink in that she finally realised what she had just done. She never thought she would be able to be that strong in a crisis, but she was proud of herself.

But then she saw him.

Alistair was sitting under the table, still paralysed by fear, in a pool of urine with melting chocolate ice-cream running down his hands. Her heart immediately sank ...

'Don't look now, but Baldy Baxter is heading this way.' Beau had true disdain in his voice.

Mr Baxter wasn't liked by anyone. He was the thirty-something-year-old vice principal whose balding hair and bad fashion made him look closer to fifty. He would constantly get snickers behind his back, and this made him rather paranoid and prone to loud outbursts. But not today, he was doing something Parker had never seen before, he was smiling.

'Oh, Parker, so glad to catch you before first period. We're going to get the big celebrity to speak at assembly today.'

'Who?' answered Parker, confused.

'Why you, of course. You're all over the news today, and we want to capitalise on that. I'm sure you'll make a wonderful speech. You've got two hours to get it ready.'

Parker knew it for sure; this was the worst day of her life.

CHAPTER THREE:
MADISON

Madison was popular, and she knew it. She seemed to lead all the trends at school, and if she changed the colour of her hair or makeup, it was guaranteed that that colour would be mirrored by many of the girls from her school the following week. She did a test once — wore the most disgusting coloured lip gloss she could find. She wore it on a Friday, and by the Monday, so many clones were wearing the same horrendous grape colour. Madison was majorly amused.

With her tight dancer's body and perfectly bleached hair, Madison looked like the all-American girl from suburban Australia. She'd even been begging her parents for a small dog she could carry around, but they always feared it would be eaten by their German shepherd, Britney. Madison liked being adored and followed by so many of the girls at her school.

But if she were popular with the girls, it was nothing compared to the attention she received from the boys. She would constantly receive anonymous emails and texts from secret admirers, and it seemed like every second boy was confessing to their friends that they were in love with her. Even worse was when they dared to declare their unrequited affections to her face.

However, Madison only had eyes for one boy: Grayson. She planned to marry him in a lavish ceremony. Yes, she may have only been fifteen, but she knew it was love. She had picked her wedding dress, a location overlooking the ocean, and she was almost through picking her bridesmaids. She would let Grayson propose on her eighteenth birthday, and they would marry a year later. Everything would be perfect.

If Madison was the Princess of the school, Grayson was the Prince. He was a member of every sporting team imaginable; the captain of most. He was a state running champion, and on weekends was a junior lifeguard. He had a tight body and was fond of showing off his growing biceps. His parents had spent a lot of money on his smile, and he knew it was worth every cent. Grayson even did quite well at school, he was not the top of the class, but he scored good enough marks to be in the top classes. And together with Madison, they truly believed they ruled the school, and that everyone loved them.

But in truth, many who copied Madison's style, resented her and were secretly jealous of her strength, her poise and her ability to be the person in the room everyone watched.

Every Princess needed a royal court, and Madison felt she had the best. While she had many friends, there were only two girls she called her best friends: Amy and Amie. Amy had Chinese heritage and was strikingly beautiful. She had always wanted to be a model, but her short height made that difficult. Amy may have been a little naïve at times, but her heart was pure, mostly.

Amie had always idolised Madison and had bleached her naturally red hair to look like her best friend, much to her mother's disappointment. Amie may not have traditionally been as thin as her two friends, but she desperately tried to stay as thin as she could. She may not have always been healthy when she did this, but she was proud to be as thin as she had ever been in her life.

Together, the three were unstoppable. Madison could rely on the pair to always be there for her, and they could rely on her to always give them advice on everything from fashion to food and fellas. Where the three girls walked, eyes would follow.

Today was like any other day at school. Peter Abrams, a Saturday afternoon larper, had told his best friend, Oliver Hunter, that he was madly in love with Madison. As Oliver himself had only last week sent Madison declarations of love on Instagram, he told the school of Peter's so-called 'little crush' on Madison. She was utterly delighted, while being suitably disgusted. The only low light for the day had been the school assembly where she was forced to sit and listen to 'the fry pan girl' stumble through some embarrassing speech.

'Anyone else would have used a knife, but not fry pan girl,' Madison commented during the speech. She was just loud enough for the four rows around her to hear and start laughing. Parker hadn't heard the comment, just the laughter, and her face turned the brightest shade of red. This made the assembled crowd laugh more. Mid-sentence, Parker uttered 'thankyou' and slunk off stage.

Amy and Amie always thought it strange that Madison loved school so much. Sure, they loved the social scene at school and had always listed lunch as their favourite subject, but they hated class and loved the end of day bell. Madison always seemed slightly upset when 3.05 arrived.

They had no idea why Madison seemed to hate going home of an afternoon. Her father was hugely successful in finance and had the pay packet, house and car to match. Her parents never seemed to fight, and they showered Madison and her brother, Lachlan, with extravagant gifts. The girls all wished they lived at the O'Sullivan palace.

Lachlan, at the tender of ten, had been diagnosed with leukemia, and the prognosis wasn't good. After several rounds of chemotherapy, Lachlan had gone into remission, and the tight knit family were relieved. However, after only a few short months, just enough time for Lachlan's hair to grow back, the cancer had returned with a vengeance. Doctors stopped using the word 'hope' and replaced it with the word 'months'. Treatment options were drying up, and they were now talking of 'making Lachlan comfortable.'

Madison was heartbroken. She loved her brother with all her heart. She'd sat at his side for endless hours at the hospital and had cried more tears than she thought she was able to produce. Her heart permanently felt dull, and she'd prayed on the hour, every hour. When Lachlan entered remission, she'd felt the greatest sense of relief, but now that his young life seemed over, she was miserable. And she hated going home. Her house had become a bleak place, and Madison didn't know how long she could continue forcing a smile when she entered her brother's bedroom. Something had to give, and Madison was scared what that might be.

She hadn't told her friends how dire things were with her brother. They knew he'd been ill, but no one knew Lachlan was close to dying. She didn't think they would understand. Amy and Amie struggled with so many things, death seemed a little beyond their limited reach. And plus, Madison didn't want to be pitied. She wanted to always be in control, and if she told anyone about Lachlan, chances were she would burst into tears, and public crying was a major faux pas. She suffered in silence, and boy was she suffering.

CHAPTER FOUR:
TINA

It had been a long day for Tina Power, the English teacher. Sure, she got to miss the double period of Year 7 English she despised so much, but a day alone on an excursion with her Year 10s was more than a little testing.

They had been studying *Romeo and Juliet* in class all term, and she had heard about a production for students in Newtown. So off they went on a bus and two trains and found themselves sitting in the smallest and grottiest theatre she had ever seen. The performances were average at best; the direction non-existent, and the set looked shabbier than the kindergarten production her son had just performed in.

To make matters worse, her students were terribly misbehaved. Madison and her friends laughed inappropriately at the women in the cast. Grayson thought it was funny to heckle Romeo during his death scene. And the Thomas twins tried to start a fight with some private school boys in the foyer. As the teachers from the other schools looked down at her with disdain, Tina had never been so embarrassed in her life.

'Excuse me, Miss, but did you understand the director's vision?'

The last thing that Tina needed was a lecture from Parker on the misgivings of the Sydney fringe theatre scene.

There was only ten minutes till the next train, and the students were all dawdling down King Street. She'd already stopped the Thomas twins from shoplifting at the local variety store. Madison and her friends had begged to stop at numerous stores and try on some clothes. Tina couldn't wait till the kids were back at school and out of her hair.

'We'll talk about it at school tomorrow,' she snapped at Parker.

'That sounds good, cause I so want to discuss why the director set the play in Paris during the 1920s and still had the cast use a mix of British and Australian accents, and that one guy with a Russian accent. Was that his real accent or was he putting it on? It sounded so average.'

'Madison O'Sullivan, are you trying to make us miss our train?' The sight of Madison ducking into a corner convenience store gave Tina the chance to escape Parker's endless questions and critiques.

'I'm getting water and gum. Would you like me to starve to death?' And with that, Madison disappeared into the store.

Tina was close to losing it. She wanted to run in and grab Madison by the hair and pull her out and make a huge example of her, but now the Thomas twins were taking off across the busy road to talk to two of the private school girls they'd been separated from in the theatre foyer.

'Parker, go in there and get Madison out of that shop. I don't care if you have to drag her out,' yelled Tina as she started across the road.

'Me? She won't listen to me.' Parker didn't want to do this at all. Madison scared the hell out of her.

'If we miss the train, I will hold you personally responsible.' Tina was off to scold the Thomas twins for the hundredth time that day, almost getting hit by the bus to Coogee while crossing the street.

Beau smiled for strength; Mel apologised with her eyes; Parker gulped. If she thought taking on the robber in her kitchen was bad, that was nothing compared to taking on Madison.

With her breath held, Parker stepped inside the grotty old convenience store. *Polite but firm* were the words that kept racing through her head. There she was, that vision of perfect hair and grooming, standing at the counter. *She's just a girl, that's all she is*, Parker told herself.

'Madison, Ms Power is going insane out there. This isn't me; she made me come in here. She's going crazy with power and is demanding you go outside now. Ms Power, crazy with power. Is that okay with you?'

There, done, it may not have been eloquent, but she didn't open her mouth and vomit — that was a good start. Parker was ready for the abuse, a death stare or even a water bottle thrown at her head. But what happened next scared the hell out of her more.

Madison turned and looked at her with apologetic eyes. It looked like she was close to tears, and Parker was confused.

That was when she saw him. A fat, ugly, sweaty man standing behind the counter with a gun pointed directly at her. Parker wondered if she was now oozing pheromones attracting lowlife criminals.

'Get inside girly, shut your pretty little mouth and you won't get hurt.'

Parker was worried for Madison; never had the self-crowned queen of the school seemed so vulnerable. If Parker wasn't so scared herself, she might be enjoying this.

'Now neither of you move or I'll shoot you both in those pretty little faces.'

Then the sweaty man started scooping money from the register into a backpack.

Instinct saw Parker moving slowly towards Madison, where she finally saw what Madison must have witnessed and why she was so scared. The shop assistant lay on the floor, unconscious, with blood pouring from his head. Parker could see he had been pistol whipped.

Parker inched closer to Madison. She felt the need to hug her, but fear stopped her reaching out. The girls kept their gaze, Madison nodding slightly, encouraging Parker to come closer to her.

The sweaty thief was now finished with the register and was busily shoving cigarette packets into his dirty old backpack. Parker was now only centimetres from Madison; Madison's eyes feverishly pleading with Parker to take the extra few steps.

'I told you little bitches not to move.' The robber turned around, backpack bulging and gun aimed squarely at Parker.

Madison dropped her bottle of water, the cracked lid leaking overpriced spring water over the old lino floor.

'So, here's where I'm supposed to shoot you, or would you just prefer I kiss you?' The robber thought this was funny; Parker thought she'd rather choose option C: vomit.

Tears started to appear in Madison's eyes, the fear was getting the better of her and Parker could hear her breathing becoming laboured. Madison was also beginning to physically crumble, her shoulders slowly starting to cave in. Parker worried Madison was not strong enough for this.

'You girls are very pretty.' The sweaty man sneered with spit foaming in the corner of his mouth. His voice became deeper, and the situation was spiralling out of control.

Parker brazenly took the extra few steps to Madison's side, who at this point had begun sobbing.

'I said not to move, you stupid little bitch.' The robber

began to pull back the trigger as his sweat dripped onto the revolver.

Madison screamed and the man began to smile.

'We have now officially missed the train, ladies, and I'm not happy.' Tina boldly stepped through the door, completely oblivious to the events inside the convenience store.

The robber turned as he was firing, the bullet ricocheting through the store.

Tina screamed; flour started to blanket the store — the bullet landing safely in the baking section.

The robber began to squeeze the trigger of his revolver again.

A panicked Tina dropped to the floor, a mix of tears and hysterics.

Without much thought, Parker and Madison held onto each other tightly.

That's when it happened.

As Parker and Madison hugged and their fingers interlaced, an exquisite blue flash of electricity shot powerfully from their hands, flying quickly through the dank air and knocked the sweaty robber off his feet.

CHAPTER FIVE:
JEREMY

Senior Constable Jeremy Hill was more than a little confused. The convenience store he always stopped at for snacks during his patrol was scorched and in shambles. Its owner, who was always good for a chat about cricket, was in hospital with concussion. Thankfully, he was alive.

The criminal who had been terrorising the shop owners of the inner west of Sydney, becoming increasingly violent, was lying in a hospital bed, bruised, burnt and with no memory of what had happened to him. The only witnesses were a petrified teacher who needed a sedative after being shot at, and two schoolgirls who seemed strangely coy. These girls had just been through a huge turmoil — a gun had been fired, they had been held hostage — yet they were sitting calmly in an interview room, sipping on bad instant coffee.

'I'm not going to have two little school girlfriends collude together and ruin my case against that criminal.' Jeremy's patience was wearing thing; these girls were telling half-truths and hiding facts.

'Let's get one thing straight, we are NOT friends. Never have been, never will be.' Madison wanted that on the record;

she didn't want people thinking she was friends with someone who dressed as badly as Parker did.

Parker smiled politely — would being friends with her be that bad?

'Hang on a second; aren't you the fry pan girl?'

Madison laughed and Parker grimaced, even strangers were recognising her. She braced herself for the jokes that were bound to follow.

'Of course, she is, don't you recognise a celebrity when you see one?' Madison was going to enjoy this. 'That's how she stopped that sweaty guy, with a fry pan. She's a one-woman fry pan vigilante.' Madison smiled; Parker did not.

'We didn't find a fry pan next to the suspect.' Jeremy could always smell a lie, and the room was getting decidedly rank.

'Well, get your CSI Newtown guys in there, because it must have been burnt up in that weird fire that started after that sweaty robber dropped his cigarette when Parker threw that fry pan and it whacked him on the head.' Madison smiled; creative writing had always been a favourite subject of hers.

It was an arrogant smile, a smile Jeremy despised.

'And that's your story too?' Jeremy turned to Parker, who just nodded.

She hated this explanation, especially because it would mean she'd never lose the 'fry pan girl' tag, but how else could she explain it? Somehow blue electricity had emitted when she and Madison touched. She wanted to reach across and touch's Madison's hand again, to see whether the beautiful blue light would return, but she was just too scared.

'It may be time to get you young ladies into separate interview rooms to find out exactly what happened, because I don't believe a word either of you are saying.'

'So, we're suspects now, are we? We must have been in on it with the sweaty fat guy. Maybe we're both in love with him and we were helping rob that ghetto convenience store. Maybe we're both pyros who love to burn tragic stores. Watch out Dotti and H&M.' Madison was also ready to get the fake tears going; they always worked on her father.

'That's not what I'm saying, but you girls aren't being truthful with me, and I really need to find out the truth.' Jeremy could feel his face going red and he hated it.

'And remember, buddy, we're both minors, and there is no way in the world my parents are going to consent to some bully boy interrogation.' Madison was now having fun. 'What's next, phone books?'

Jeremy was just getting ready to lose it when he heard a disruption outside. A woman ranting. Jeremy thought that crazy Mavis, the homeless woman convinced that Oprah Winfrey was having her followed, was back again with some new insane conspiracy theory. But then the door burst open, and people started piling into the room. His sergeant had that look on his face that always scared Jeremy; he looked ready to kill someone. Jeremy knew that soon he would feel the force of that anger.

'I am going to call my lawyer and we are going to sue every person who has even stepped into this God-awful place.' Madison's mum was unstoppable; people cowered in fear at her office, and she relished seeing powerful men crumble before her. 'These poor girls have been through a huge turmoil, and you start interrogating minors without their parents. Do you want me to just take your badges now?'

The dialogue continued; the constable made excuses, apologised and tried to shove the girls out the door.

Madison's mum continued her tirade with the occasional backing vocals from Parker's mum. The girls' fathers didn't need to speak; they knew their wives were better than them at confrontations — they both knew that only too well.

Jeremy kept repeating that all he was trying to do was find out what really happened, but it was lost in the hurrah.

And through it all, Parker and Madison stared at each other. They knew they'd be departing within minutes, and their parents wouldn't be leaving them alone for a second. They hadn't had a moment alone since they somehow conducted electricity together. As soon as the bullets had been fired and the fires began, their classmates had run through the door. First was Griffin, the strangely handsome and quiet boy who barely socialised. He was ready to help his classmates in whatever way he could. Second was Beau, panicked, ready to protect Parker with all his might. Grayson didn't quite make it through the door; he had plenty of convincing reasons why when asked later.

Soon enough, the police arrived and had not given them a moment alone. Madison had started talking, making up stories, and Parker just followed along. Both desperately wanted to ask a million questions of each other, but now they were walking out of the police station into waiting cars.

Both mothers had barely calmed down, now focusing attention on their respective daughters, asking the same question in a hundred different ways: 'Are you okay?'

The girls barely answered, instead watching each other until their cars pulled away. This had been the most unbelievable day of their lives, but they couldn't tell a soul.

That night, Madison's mum looked through the door every hour on the hour.

Parker's mum slept in the bed next to Parker.

But neither Parker nor Madison slept — they just stared at their fingers, waiting for more electricity to flow out.

CHAPTER SIX:
PARKER & MADISON

Today had been another bad one for Parker. People didn't even pretend they weren't looking anymore; they just openly gawked at her, and most pointed as she walked past. For a girl who liked to fly under the radar, she was now the most talked about person at the whole school. People who barely mumbled a word to her in the past, now suddenly wanted a chat. A little Year 7 boy who was being bullied even tried to hire Parker as his heavy, but all she wanted was Beau and Mel, and that allusive conversation with Madison, who seemed to be avoiding her.

Madison, on the other hand, was enjoying the attention. She loved that more people were now in awe of her — her infamy was building. She relished recounting exactly what happened as scores of people surrounded her and hung off every word. So what if the story changed a little bit each time? No one was going to question her now — she'd stopped a wanted sweaty criminal; she was a hero.

Parker and Madison passed once in the playground before school. Parker smiled; she was hoping this was when they would finally have a talk about what happened.

Madison, however, quickly turned her head. She was

already engrossed in a conversation on how her quick-thinking saved the day.

Ms Power was still off sick — Madison telling everyone she'd been shipped off to a psych ward — so Baldy Baxter was taking English for the day. Parker was desperate to talk about the average theatre performance from the day before, but everyone else, especially Baldy Baxter, wanted to talk about the other 'spectacle'.

Madison jumped to the front of the classroom when asked; Parker needing to be persuaded. Madison again relished her opportunity to lie with great flair to an assembled mass. Madison even heard Parker snarl and grimace when she said to the class, 'The guy was pointing the gun at Ms Power, and then I saw a fry pan next to Parker and I told her to pick it up and throw it, cause she's good at that.'

The fifty-minute period felt like hours to Parker, and Mr Baxter dedicated the entire class to the girls' heroics. When the bell finally rang for recess, Parker jumped from her seat and almost bolted from the class.

Recess was just as painful. Parker made Beau and Mel hang out with her behind the assembly hall until the Thomas twins arrived to sneak some cigarettes and started to taunt Parker with unimaginative jokes about fry pans. It was still only morning, and Parker was sure the end of day would never arrive.

By the time recess ended, Parker was running very late for History, and Mrs Ling was not going to put up with any excuses. At least Parker knew Mrs Ling wouldn't make her talk in front of the class. She'd just remind her that in her class everyone was the same and no five minutes of fame was going to make her special in her eyes, and that's exactly what Parker wanted to hear. Parker was running down the hallway, she was alone since Beau and Mel had Commerce, when she was grabbed from behind and pulled into the staff toilets.

There was no scream; it was more of a whimper. But when Parker turned, ready to face who ever grabbed her, she was ready for a fight. The past week had taught her just how strong she was. She raised her hands into fists, ready for anything.

'You going to punch me now, are you?' Madison stood bathed in the glow of the fluorescent light above her. She seemed both angelic and demonic, all at the same time.

Parker quickly dropped her fists as Madison locked the door behind them; Madison didn't want anyone seeing them together.

'So, you're going to talk to me now, are you?' Parker was like a petulant child.

'We spoke in English at the front of the class.' Madison knew what Parker meant, but she wasn't going to tell her that the two of them talking was popularity suicide. 'But this has just answered every question I had. I touched you and there were no sparks. It was just some freak accident in that shop. We can go.' Madison headed for the door, unlocking it; she just hoped that no one would see her exit with Parker.

'Hang on a second, Madison. When we were in that store, our hands touched. You only touched my clothing then.'

Madison turned back around, letting go of the door handle. 'So ... you think that we could do it again, we could make that blue light?'

'Maybe, who would have thought it would happen the first time?'

'Well let's call in Mr Anderson; he flunked me on my Maths exam last week. We'll give him a quick jolt.'

'But what was it, that electricity? It came from us; it came from inside us.'

Madison didn't know.

The girls stared at each other. They tried to read the other, but all they could focus on was their own confusion. Neither wanted to believe what had happened. Madison didn't want to be different, and she didn't want to be seen as a freak. Parker had just wanted to get through school with her head down. She'd received more attention than she ever wanted, and if it was discovered she was a walking talking electricity conductor, her life would be all but over.

Without words, the girls put their hands out, fingers extended, slowly moving so their fingers could meet. They were both nervous, unsure what would happen next. Holding their breaths, the girls moved closer, extending their hands even further. Parker wanted to close her eyes as the girls softly let their fingers touch. Madison was ready for another explosion, but all that happened was nothing. No electricity, no fire. Nothing.

'I should have known, nothing. I should never have let you get carried away with this ridiculousness.' Madison was upset; part of her wanted there to be a spark. But there was also the relief that she no longer shared a bond with Parker.

Suddenly, the door flung open.

Brooding Griffin entered the room, shocked to see someone else in the toilet. He quickly apologised and started to back out of the room, but then he caught sight of a stunning blue light radiating from the fingers of Parker and Madison. The blue light shot to the roof and smouldered, leaving a black scorch mark on the ceiling and setting off the fire alarms.

The girls immediately snatched away their hands, placing them squarely behind their backs.

'What the hell was that?' Griffin smiled; it was the most beautiful light he'd seen in his life. He was not shocked or scared, just intrigued.

'This dweeb here was trying to learn how to smoke and I busted her, told her only idiots smoke and her lighter must have exploded,' Madison said, trying to come up with any plausible excuse.

'That wasn't a lighter exploding, it was too beautiful, and I don't see a lighter. Come on, you can trust me, what was it?' Griffin was a believer in the supernatural. He believed that people could perform magic, he just never thought it would happen at his school. Especially by someone like Madison, who he thought was vacuous.

The noise of students exiting their classrooms was building. Most students believed this was just another fire drill, so they were slowly making their way to the sports oval, followed by teachers who were upset their lessons were interrupted by another ridiculous fire drill.

'What would you know anyway? There's a fire drill on, and we'll get in trouble if we miss it.' Madison grabbed her bag and moved towards the door. There were too many questions that hadn't been answered, especially the one about her hanging out with Parker.

Griffin wouldn't move, he was blocking the door. He didn't care about some silly fire alarm; he knew there was no fire — it had disappeared into the ceiling after shooting from the hands of two girls he never spoke to at school. He looked at Parker, who just looked lost, unable to speak.

Madison, with hand outstretched, went to push past Griffin. But as her hand connected to his, a small blue light radiated between them. It was not as strong as the light that had omitted from the girls, and it seemed to hang in the air, like a balloon, before evaporating into nothing. But all three saw the light generate and disappear.

Parker gasped; Griffin smiled at Madison, and Madison ran from the room.

CHAPTER SEVEN:
GRIFFIN

'How about we just leave the door open?' Madison's dad said as he let Grayson into Madison's room.

Madison wanted to answer back, but she didn't. Grayson may look hot in his short-sleeved shirt, but she was still annoyed that he hadn't quite made it into the convenience store to see if she was okay. And plus, she couldn't decide if she was annoyed or relieved that he didn't want to hear anything more about the infamous convenience store incident.

Even with the door open, Grayson was feeling comfortable. He kicked his shoes off and lay next to Madison on the bed. He began to kiss her neck; this was a game Madison usually loved. He would try to push the boundaries and Madison would resist. She liked the idea of driving him crazy and then making him wait. But not tonight — she was in no mood for power struggles and got straight up and sat behind her desk.

Grayson sat up in disgust and fixed his shirt, which he'd managed to strategically open, revealing the emerging six pack he had been working on. But unfortunately, Madison hadn't even noticed. 'Well, why did I even come over if we aren't going to at least make out?' Grayson was not used to being ignored.

Madison was certainly over Grayson for the night. She still wanted to marry him, she'd made notes about the catering in her wedding journal that day, but tonight she wanted him out of mind, and more importantly, out of sight. 'I was hoping you came over to see me, and I don't feel like making out. I nearly died this week, and you seem more interested in giving me a hickey.'

Grayson vehemently denied he had no interest, but Madison kept pushing for more attention. Grayson took his shirt completely off. Madison's dad walked past, saw Grayson's naked torso and threw him out of the room. Madison pretended to argue, but she was relieved.

Madison then lay on her bed; sleep was far from her thoughts. She contemplated whether to call Amy or Amie when she was startled by a knock at her window. She jumped up, angry at being scared and even angrier that Grayson was trying to sneak back in. She ripped open the curtain, ready to yell at him, loud enough for her father to hear.

But it was not Grayson trying to get back in, it was Parker. Parker looked nervously around, making sure no one had seen her.

Madison felt a great sense of relief, unsure whether it was because a half-naked Grayson wasn't there, or because she really did want to see Parker. The one thing she knew she didn't want was anyone seeing her *with* Parker. 'Go to the park down the end of my street. I'll be there in ten minutes.'

'But it's really dark in that park,' pleaded Parker. She'd always hated that park; it was scary at night.

'Exactly.' Without waiting for an answer, Madison ripped close the curtains. She turned on her game face and went to complain to her mother that her father had thrown out the love of her life. Pretty soon she had her mum convinced that her dad had overreacted, and she should go off and chase Grayson, to see if he was okay. So with a quick kiss to her brother on the way out the door, Madison headed to the park.

Parker sat on a swing, scared to do more than lightly swing while continually looking over her shoulder. It was late, it was dark, and the moon was veiled by ominous-looking clouds. The slide next to her was covered with graffiti, and the light in the park flickered slightly. Parker was sure she'd seen this exact scene in that slasher film Beau made her watch two weekends before. She wished she was somewhere else and not waiting for someone who'd always been a stranger to her.

Parker heard someone approaching the park. She turned sharply, holding her breath in anticipation. She sighed with relief when she saw it was Madison. She smiled widely, a smile so warm and infectious that Madison was suddenly glad she'd come, even though she had considered leaving Parker alone at the park.

'What are we going to do?' It was all Madison could ask.

Parker's response was quick and decisive, 'We have to find some way to figure this thing out.'

Madison mumbled an agreement under her breath and then the unlikely pair continued to eyeball each other. Neither had an answer nor a credible theory, at least one they wanted to share. The silence continued, though not uncomfortably. They felt safe together and without words — they had become confidants.

Both girls turned suddenly when they heard a stick snapping. Then they turned to each other and instinctively held out their hands, ready to touch if they needed. Both girls realised what they'd done, but instead of pulling away, they found solace and strength.

'Who's there?' questioned Parker.

'Tell us who it is, or you will regret it big time.' Madison was enjoying her taste of power.

'Don't shoot; I know what you can do with those hands.' And with that, Griffin stepped out, his jet-black hair glistening in the moonlight.

'Are you following us?' Madison was trialling out her 'tough voice', and she liked the result.

Griffin explained he lived around the corner and had seen Parker walking towards Madison's house, and suspected they had been practising their art. 'What are you both, witches?'

The girls underestimated what Griffin saw in the staff toilet, and they were quickly discovering he had quite the imagination.

'No! We were doing our Chemistry prac down here.' Madison was finding storytelling easier and easier.

Parker smiled in agreement.

'I saw you both performing some kind of magic. And you cast something on me too. It was the coolest thing I've ever seen.'

'And how many people have you told?' Madison was back to being firm.

Parker was just panicking; she hadn't considered he would have told anyone.

·'No one, I promise. Who would I tell?'

Parker felt bad when she realised Griffin had two less friends than her.

'So, you didn't hop on some loser Twitter thread and tell a bunch of freaks on the other side of the globe that you have proof of something you didn't even see?' Madison was less trusting than Parker.

'I knew you wouldn't want this out,' Griffin pleaded. 'You're right to keep it quiet.'

Parker believed him, and surprisingly, so did Madison.

'Then why are you here?' Madison questioned.

Griffin had chosen to be a loner. There was a time he was just like the pack, but his different tastes started to separate him from the others when he hit high school. He lost the urge to play sport, and his father had never fully forgiven him for giving up his burgeoning career in soccer. When he stopped returning his friend's calls and didn't turn up to social gatherings, his friends didn't understand and cut him loose, but he'd found something else.

Griffin had always been close with his grandmother. His first memory was sitting in the backyard watching her build a shed. She was a woman who'd lost her husband early and had done it all alone. She oozed strength, and Griffin idolised her. Their bond was so strong that she couldn't bring herself to let her favourite grandchild know her heart was ready to give out. And so, in the holidays between primary school and high school, while other kids enjoyed their summer, Griffin lost his nana. It changed him.

He became a darker child, obsessed with the supernatural. He had seen the film *The Sixth Sense* and believed if he tried hard enough, he could see his grandmother again. He began to hold séances — the last of his friends were scared off by those. He never managed to contact his beloved grandmother, but it never stopped him from believing. And now at last, he had proof of something supernatural, and for the first time in years, he had hope.

Griffin was tall for his age with deep-set eyes. His parents had met in Vietnam — his father was on holidays when he fell in love with the young woman who was serving him drinks in the local bar. They had stayed in touch, and their love had grown through letters. Within a year, they had married, and she moved to Australia. Griffin came that following year, cementing their love. His parents loved him and tried to understand why he was now so distant. They were often left worrying about their moody and quiet son.

Parker felt a sudden ease with Griffin; she sensed he was a kindred spirit. So, without thought, she started to tell Griffin all that had happened to the pair. Madison tried to stop her, but once Parker started, she couldn't stop. She couldn't only share this secret with Madison, someone she was pretty sure hated her.

'And what causes the blue lightning?' asked Griffin. He was dying to see another example of the girls' magic, and even more, he wanted to see if he could conduct electricity again.

'If we knew, do you think we'd be down here in the dark of night like a bunch of freaks?' Madison was frank.

They talked in circles for another ten minutes, but all anyone wanted to see was whether the girls could create the beautiful blue light again. Soon the girls were stepping closer together, hands stretching to touch, slightly reluctant. All three held their breaths as the girls again attempted to touch.

But there was nothing.

'I can't believe I let you freaks let me think I was some kind of superhero. I'm going home.' Madison turned and started to walk away in a huff.

Parker pleaded. She and Griffin chased Madison, but she was building momentum and was almost out of the darkened park.

'I know why it didn't work', Griffin said.

Parker turned to face him

Madison stopped walking. 'If this is some stupid trick you saw on some crap TV show, I will find a way to generate electricity and shoot you straight in the —'

'What is it, Griffin?' Parker interrupted Madison.

'Both times you've done it, you had heightened emotion. You were scared and it protected you. It must work from the way you're feeling.'

'All right, Einstein, what about you and me? We made a spark, and I certainly wasn't scared of you?' Madison didn't want to acknowledge that Griffin had come up with an idea she hadn't.

'You were scared, scared of being caught. But anger was your main emotion, and it was heightened. As for me, I was pretty damn pumped about what I saw.'

'It makes sense.' For Parker, this was the closest thing to reason she'd heard since this ordeal had begun.

Madison was silent — she didn't want to agree, but Griffin's theory seemed to hold weight.

Soon the three were again standing under the flickering light in the park. The girls were holding hands and trying to make themselves angry or scared, but nothing was working.

Madison was getting annoyed again, and Parker was starting to lose hope, but it was Griffin who still pushed.

'Just imagine, Madison, if Grayson and those bimbo Amys walked into the park right now and saw you here with me and holding hands with Parker. Imagine what they'd say and what would happen when they tell the school we were your best friends now? And Parker, I saw your face at school during those speeches you had to make. Or should I just call you "fry pan girl"?'

Without warning, the beautiful blue light began to return. It started deep from within the girls; Griffin saw a brief blue glaze wash over the girls' eyes. Their fingertips started to glow, and soon a beautiful blue jet was radiating from their joined hands.

'Griffin, put your hands on,' Parker urged.

Griffin didn't need to be told twice. This was the happiest he'd been in his entire time at high school.

Parker too was excited, and Madison, even though the word '*freak*' echoed in her head, was astounded at how much joy this moment was providing.

The beam of electricity flickering between the girls was intense, and when Griffin placed his hand on Parker's, nothing happened. His heart immediately sank; he was not special like the girls.

'It was Madison you had the connection with last time, try her,' added Parker, and Griffin moved his hands to Madison's. Immediately a huge bolt of lightning emitted from the three, setting a tall eucalyptus tree alight. The three smiled, still unsure why this was happening, but glad it had. It was something very wonderful indeed.

In the distance, they heard an old women's voice scream out to her husband about hoodlums and calling the fire brigade.

The three ran, sated for now — content they were starting to control this amazing ability that had seemingly laid dormant inside them.

CHAPTER EIGHT:
THE THOMAS TWINS

The Thomas twins were annoyed as they waited for the fire brigade and the police to leave their park. They'd arrived to see the large, majestic eucalyptus tree in flames and managed to just duck into the scrub when they heard the sirens turn into the street. They always waited till their alcoholic father was passed out on the floor and then simply walked out the front door to the safety of their domain. No one ever came to their park after dark, except for tonight.

'When I find out who's been lighting fires in our park, they're dead,' whispered Arlo to his brother Devon, who nodded in agreement.

Arlo was half an hour older than Devon, and that's pretty much where the differences ended. Wherever you found one, you would find the other. The identical twins looked rough and almost indistinguishable, except for some small variances. Arlo was a few centimetres taller, and Devon's face was slightly rounder — but people could barely tell them apart.

Their clothes rarely seemed to be washed, and their brown hair was unkept and oily. But the distinct lack of food at their house, and their tendency to ride their skateboards for hours, left a slender frame that many girls secretly admired. Both had been in trouble with the police before — always minor crimes: underage drinking, shoplifting, and they'd started several fights at the local skate park. The authorities had been to their rundown house many times before, and their father was threatened with losing the boys, but he never took the threats seriously. Plus, his life would probably be easier if they were gone.

'Did anyone check if we had any lightning tonight?' asked the police officer as he left the park, looking to the dark clouds. The 000 call was just another from old Frida with the bad wig, but this time she really did see a fire. However, the fireys saw no evidence of arson and the police were satisfied the whole thing was a freak accident.

As the fire engines and police squad cars began to drive away, Arlo and Devon stepped out from the shadows, annoyed it was almost midnight and they hadn't done anything tonight.

'About time they left,' said a female now entering from the other side of the scrub.

The twins turned to see Amie walking across to them. Even late at night and after hiding in the wilderness, Amie still looked like the cover of a teen magazine with her perfect hair, makeup and designer clothes — clothes Madison picked out for her on their last shopping trip.

'I would have thought the pigs would have scared you off?' Arlo smiled at Amie.

Her grin back was even bigger. 'Never, baby'.

The pair leaned in and began to kiss passionately. As they did, a dark-blue light began to glow from their joined lips. It hovered around their faces, illuminating their kiss. The light didn't dissipate until the pair stopped kissing. All Arlo could mutter was 'Hot', while Amie smiled wickedly.

Devon was feeling concerned. 'You aren't with Mel?'

Amie could only shake her head.

'I'm here.' Mel crawled out of the scrub, covered in dirt and leaves, not far from where the boys had been seeking refuge. She didn't look as glamorous as Amie. Her hair had a few twigs protruding from the abundance of dark-brown curls.

'I would have thought the cops would have scared you off?' snarled Amie. Mel may have joined their secret group to be with Devon, but that didn't mean Amie had to like her.

Mel hadn't noticed Amie's tone; she was too busy brushing off the mess that covered her. She went on to explain she had wanted to leave, but she was scared. She had heard the boys nearby but was frozen to the spot and couldn't think about moving.

In the dark, no one could see Amie roll her eyes.

Mel continued to tell of her fear of being caught until Devon stopped her with a kiss. And just like his brother, the same dark-blue light hung around their mouths as his tongue explored Mel's. Their kiss seemed to go on longer than the other pair and was only stopped by Arlo, who was quickly growing impatient and ready to share his plan.

It had always just been the twins, they never needed anyone else. Other people asked them too many questions, like why their mother had been in jail for so long. Plus, the twins barely needed to communicate; they weren't big on words, and when it was just them, they could speak without saying anything. They'd never planned on getting themselves involved with anyone else, but this was more than just getting girlfriends; this was about something very special indeed.

It began with Amie. She'd lived around the corner from the boys all her life. And while Madison told her they were to be avoided, she couldn't help but be intrigued by them. Madison decided Amie should be dating Henry, one of Grayson's friends. But Henry wasn't very smart and was starting to develop back hair. He'd declared his love and told her he wanted to marry her someday, and she went along with it. But the closer Henry tried to get, the more attracted to Arlo she became. He was her favourite, not for looks, the brothers were the same. But for attitude. He was the leader of the pair, and he had a strength Amie admired, probably because it was a strength she lacked.

Amie began to follow the boys late at night. When she would see them walk past after dark, she would carefully take down her fly screen and crawl through the window. She would watch them get up to trouble; she lived vicariously through their rebellious antics. When they were breaking factory windows with empty bottles, she felt as if she was the one brandishing the bottle. She felt invigorated and mischievous, that was until she was caught one night.

The boys hurried around a corner; Amie rushed to catch them, and they were waiting for her, aware they were being followed. She made some pathetic excuse and began to cry. The boys were never going to hurt her, but they wanted to make her think they would. Devon held her at first as Arlo put the fear of God into her.

But it was when Arlo grabbed her, ready to push her away, that the beautiful dark-blue streak of lightning jettisoned from their connected skin and burst a shop window. After grabbing the contents from the window display in the camping store, Arlo and Amie would meet every night to try and harness their new-found ability.

Devon began feeling left out and was campaigning for Arlo to cut Amie loose. They had never kept girlfriends before, and Devon didn't want them to start now. But Arlo wasn't ready to let his new-found power go, and he decided that if he had found a way to have a special power with a local girl, then there must also be a matching girl for his brother. Never before had they been different.

So, a hunt began for a girl who could literally cause a lightning field with Devon. The boys figured raw emotion was the trigger, so they started provoking all the girls in their school. If they were feared before, now they were just plain scary. They'd follow the girls from school, and when one was all alone, they'd scare her. Devon would then grab their hand.

However, there was no blue light.

Then they'd tell the girl she wasn't who they wanted and would run off. The girls were usually so relieved to be let go and scared of repercussions that they stayed silent.

They were getting desperate by the time they reached Mel. It was Parker that Devon had originally hoped was his match. He had always thought she was cute — nerdish, but cute. And when the fry pan incident occurred, he liked her strength and desperately wanted her to be his partner.

That day after school, the boys followed Parker, but she was always surrounded by Beau and Mel. When Parker invited Beau into her house, the twins realised that there wasn't a chance to test Parker's abilities. So instead, they thought they'd rule Mel out of contention.

Mel always took a shortcut home through an alleyway. The fences were covered in graffiti, empty beer bottles lay on the floor, and Mel's mum had warned her not to walk through it. However, Mel went that way everyday with her phone playing Ariana Grande into her air buds. She was singing under her breath, and the last thing she expected was a hand grabbing her mouth from behind. She tried to scream, but the sound wouldn't come out. There was a whisper she barely heard about not being hurt and a hand reaching down and touching hers. Before her mind could race to worst-case scenarios, a beautiful dark-blue light shot from her hands, knocking her and the Thomas twins to the floor.

Devon's search was complete.

Mel had never felt special in her life. No boy had ever shown interest in her, and she even felt like an outsider with her friends. She'd always thought if she stopped coming to school that Parker and Beau wouldn't notice for at least a week. It wasn't that she felt ugly, she just felt plain. She would look in the mirror and curse that she didn't look like Madison, her friends, or even like Parker. So, when she shared such an intense connection with Devon, she finally felt important. The boys, in particular Devon, needed her. She found it easy to fall in love with him, and even easier to betray her closest friends for a secret pact with the twins.

After more practise in the darkened park, the foursome strode into the night, heads high and full of self-importance. They were on a mission.

Beside Amie's occasional protests of the boys flirting with girls at the recent tragic theatre excursion, the walk was a quiet one. What they were about to embark on was the first real test for the group, and they were determined to not only have it work, but not to get caught.

The twins had spent the past few days casing the area. They were going to target the pedestrian mall, but they realised that cameras lazily strewn through the area could catch them performing the act that was going to make them rich. But they soon discovered, just outside the big shopping complex, there was an ATM that had a camera positioned directly on it, but no camera surrounding it. So, they thought that this was the perfect target.

The four stood in a line, the boys standing tall and smiling proudly at each other. The girls were nervous, but didn't want to show it, particularly to each other. A light wind was blowing, and it only seemed to add to the nervous energy in the air. Without much warning, Arlo grabbed Amie's hand, a blue light beginning to buzz around them. Devon turned to

Mel and smiled as he took her hand, the blue light also dancing around their joined hands. The boys then looked at each other.

'You ready, bro?' Arlo asked his brother, who smiled in return.

They joined hands and in no time at all, the dark-blue lightning shot through their bodies and out of the boy's hands. Immediately, the ATM short circuited and the screen began to burn. Hands were dropped and the boys retrieved balaclavas from their pockets.

The alarm in the bank began to sound, and the girls felt their first tinges of panic. But not the boys, they were soon pulling apart the ATM, which now predominately lay on the floor in a broken mess. They scooped all the cash they could into a bag and within two minutes were sprinting down the street with the girls in tow, richer than they'd ever been in their lives.

CHAPTER NINE:
BEAU

Saturdays for Parker and Beau had become 'their' day. Sometimes they ventured into the world, but they seemed happiest holed up in each other's bedrooms. Sometimes they would be joined by Mel, and even though they would never admit it, they preferred when it was just the two of them. Mel was due that day but had text her apologies; she was spending the day with her mum.

Sundays were spent doing homework, usually over the phone with each other, but Saturday was reserved for their own private universe. Parker's parents and Beau's mum had often wondered what happened behind closed doors, but as soon as they entered the room, the pair would go quiet. It was here, in the safety of their own domains, that they took on the world and made plans for the future.

Today was no different. The pair had discussed anything and everything, including the future and the past, but the present was a noticeable exception. It seemed that something was holding both Parker and Beau back. The conversation certainly flowed, but both felt an uneasiness and knew they needed to talk. They didn't like to keep secrets from each other, and both had a big one that was eating away at them.

The night of the convenience store hold-up, Beau was waiting on Parker's front doorstep when she arrived home, desperate to make sure she was all right. She'd wanted to tell him what had happened, but what could she say when she wasn't even sure what had really taken place?

Then there was the encounter in the staff toilet. By that stage, Parker was certain this wasn't just some freak incident. She was ready to tell Beau; it couldn't possibly be true until she told him. But how? She spent that afternoon skirting around the issue. Every time she tried to tell him, something else would come out. She ended up telling him she'd spoken to Griffin so many times, Beau was probably beginning to think that she must like him.

But after last night, when Madison, Griffin and herself had set a tree alight with their hands, Parker knew she had to tell her best friend.

However, Beau had a secret of his own that had been eating away at him long before Parker had discovered she could conduct electricity. This was a deep secret that he'd tried to deny to himself. He had his own ball of fire growing inside of him, and he couldn't contain it any longer. Parker was the only person he trusted, and he felt he was not being a true friend by keeping it from her.

But Parker got in first.

Parker was on her third coffee for the day, and it was only 11.30am. She skulled the remaining unsugared black liquid from her cup, took a deep breath and knew it was time.

'Beau, we need to talk,' she solemnly told him.

His heart sank. He knew what this was about. He nodded in agreement.

She continued, 'There's something very serious happening. We have never kept secrets before, and I feel sick that there's a secret now.' Parker's guilt was eating away at her, but just as she was about to launch into an explanation, she noticed her best friend's face.

A tear rolled slowly down his cheek.

Before she could even ask what was wrong, he was standing, heading for the corner, hiding his face. Normally, she would think it looked comical that a tall boy like Beau was using a small teddy bear to cover his face. His dark-blonde hair protruding behind the brown bear. She could hear him crying, and she was at a loss. Parker hadn't seen Beau this upset since his father left. It had been four years. Parker had never seen Beau's parents argue; in fact, she thought they had the perfect marriage. Her own parents, despite their wonderful qualities, always took at least an hour out of every week to have a loud fight. So, when Beau's folks decided to part ways, it not only surprised Parker, but floored Beau. He was devastated, and part of him had never recovered.

Parker raced straight over to him. She tried to hug him, but he pulled away.

He was upset and embarrassed and wasn't quite sure how Parker knew his secret.

She pleaded with him to let her in, but he kept his head turned firmly away. Finally, she managed to take his hand, and she was not going to let it go, no matter how hard he fought. She kept repeating his name, both firmly and lovingly until he finally turned and held her tightly. And as she held him, she whispered to him, 'Please, Beau, tell me what's happening?'

Beau looked up at her, his eyes red and face tear stained. 'But how did you know? Does everyone know?'

Parker knew that Beau couldn't be talking about her new-found strength. Had she been so caught up with Madison, someone she didn't even like, that she'd failed to see the problems of her best friend? 'I'm not leaving this room until you tell me what's wrong.'

She meant it, and Beau knew it. As hard as this was, he knew what he had to do. He gathered all his courage, looked at Parker with dread and uttered the words, 'I'm gay'. And then suddenly Beau felt a wave of relief run over him. This had been buried so deep that it had slowly been eating away at him. But by telling his best friend, he felt free.

Part of Parker was shocked, but she was also relieved nothing was seriously wrong. The thought had crossed her mind before; he'd certainly been teased enough by the idiot boys at school, but she'd never given it much serious thought. Parker had heard him be called, 'camp' and 'fairy', and hated that sometimes she could see him try to act more masculine for others. She was never particularly interested in romance and never discussed it; she just thought Beau was the same. She was more upset that she'd failed to see something so important.

The pair began to talk, nothing was left unsaid. Beau confessed his thoughts, he smiled, and Parker knew the relief he must be feeling. Beau talked about how alone he had truly felt; that no one could understand what he was really feeling, and that his own feelings seemed to turn against him. He talked about telling his parents someday and how they might react. He even mentioned a crush he had, but that could wait for another day — he wasn't quite ready to empty all the eggs from his basket.

Parker tried to pry it out of him, but he wasn't going to let that one budge ... for now.

At the end of the day, as Parker left to head home and to have dinner with her family, Beau hugged Parker tighter than ever before. He looked her directly in the eyes, smiled and thanked her for being the best friend he could ever have. He told her he loved her and that without her, he would be a mess.

As she walked home, Parker was delighted that she now felt closer to Beau; however, part of her was upset because she just couldn't tell Beau about her secret, and she hated herself for it.

CHAPTER TEN:
BALDY BAXTER

Parker was a fan of routine, and there was nothing routine about the past week. A new week held promise, and she was determined to return to whatever normality she could muster. So far, so good. Her double period of Maths almost bored her to sleep, and at recess everyone returned to ignoring her. Two Year 9 girls had both discovered they kissed the same boy and decided to fight it out in the playground. The fight had been recorded on multiple phones, and the footage was being sent many times around the school. Parker passed those who had been whispering about her on Friday; they were now ignoring her again and talking about the broken wrist one of the Year 9 girls had suffered. This made her smile.

Now Parker was sitting in her favourite subject: English. Madison turned her back on her as she stepped into class. Griffin briefly smiled, but he sat on the other side of the room, alone. Parker was sitting with Beau, who smiled and thanked her quietly for Saturday. Mel was beside him. They were discussing *Romeo and Juliet* in class today. Ms Power was back and didn't want to talk about the robbery at all. The Thomas twins kept teasing her and asking her if she needed to change her underwear after the ill-fated event in the convenience store. But once they'd been sent to Mr Baxter's office, things got back to routine.

Parker foolishly believed that things were back to normal again.

The Thomas twins were regulars in the office of the Vice Principal. Last week they'd been sent to the office from History. Mrs Ling was one tough cookie; she barely showed emotion and was known to turn tough kids into quivering messes. The boys dared each other to see who could make her cry first. After weeks of trying, the winner was naturally Arlo. Mrs Ling was left sobbing in front of a stunned class, and the boys were given one last warning: if they were sent to the office again, they'd be suspended.

The boys nervously entered the office; they knew Mr Baxter was not one for idle threats. And after the fight in the playground that morning, he was at the end of his tether. The second Devon closed the door behind them, Baldy Baxter was off. He was ranting and raving so much that his bald head went a deep shade of red.

The boys tried to make excuses, could Ms Power be suffering from post-traumatic stress syndrome? But nothing worked, and the boys were suspended for two weeks. Normally this would mean nothing to them, but the school dance was the following week, and their suspension included all school activities. The Thomas twins' main money spinner, before their new ATM robberies, was to sell alcohol to underage kids at school. Their cousin worked at a local bottle shop and would always help them out with any orders they had. The school disco was their biggest payday, but now thanks to Baldy Baxter, they were out on the street and out of pocket.

Back in English class, Parker was reading the play aloud when Amie made some disparaging comment about Parker, but it wasn't Ms Power who told her to be quiet, it was Madison. Parker smiled, maybe knowing Madison wasn't such a bad thing. Amie questioned why Madison would defend a dork, and Madison shut her down even quicker by reminding her of her father's recent rant about grades and the withholding of money for an end of year trip with her friends.

Amie stewed in her seat; she pretended she was following Madison blindly like Amy always did, but really, she wished that Arlo was in the class right now. She would be tempted to reach across, grab his hand and send an electricity bolt straight to Madison's perfect hair and then see how she liked public embarrassment.

At first, Amie was so deep in thoughts of revenge that she didn't even see the Year 7 boy enter the class with a note in his hand. It wasn't till the whole class was looking at her, and Madison was making some joke about her having nothing inside her head, that she realised Ms Power was talking to her.

'Amie French, did you hear me? You and Mel have been called to Mr Baxter's office.'

Amie muttered 'What?', which sent the class into huge laughter. Soon she was standing and ready to storm out of the class. In this moment, she hated them all.

Mel stood, unsure of what was happening. Had they been caught? She looked worried, and Parker whispered to her that everything would be all right. But Parker didn't have a clue about what she was going through. Mel walked out of the room, with panic beginning to consume her.

'Do they know?' Mel asked Amie when she finally caught up to her descending the stairs.

'What did I say about speaking to me in public?' was

Amie's only response, but she was thinking the same thing. Her father would never let her go out again if she were arrested.

The girls nervously walked towards Baldy Baxter's office, the Year 7 kid walking in front of them. Mel wanted to ask the kid if there were police officers waiting for them, but she was scared of the answer.

Before they could enter the administration building, a hand grabbed them both from behind. The girls let out small, scared noises, but it was the small messenger who seemed the most frightened when he saw the Thomas twins grabbing the girls.

'Here's your EpiPen back, and if you mention to anyone what you did today, I'm gonna steal it again and shove a peanut butter sandwich straight down your throat. We clear?'

The kid nodded his head at Arlo; he knew this wasn't just a threat to scare him, this could very well be his demise. With tears of joy in his eyes, he took his EpiPen and went to go hide in the toilets. He wished he were back in primary school.

The girls were full of questions for the boys, but they were mostly just relieved that it was the twins that had gotten them pulled from class. The girls kept asking what was happening and what the plan was.

The boys were quiet and smiling; they had a devious scheme and needed the girls' help to set it in motion.

Back in class, it was Amy's turn to read in front of the class. No matter how much protesting she'd done, Ms Power was determined to hear her read. Amy was even more resistant when she heard she would be reading a monologue from the Nurse character in *Romeo and Juliet*. Amy made a disclaimer that at no point in her actual life would she ever be a nurse. Ms Power threatened to make her stay during the lunch break, and Amy quickly began. Amy was not a good reader at the best of times, but her rendition of Shakespearean prose was painful.

Amy stumbled through the words, every second sentence corrected by Ms Power.

Parker's mind was starting to wander. She looked across to Griffin, who was staring back at her. She could tell he wished he was sitting at her table instead of sitting alone, but she still wasn't able to explain to Beau what was happening. She also looked across at Madison, who was trying to stop Grayson from laughing at Amy's poor script delivery. She was ready to turn back when Madison looked straight at her and smiled. As quickly as she had smiled, Madison turned her focus back to Grayson, but it had been enough for Parker. The smile made her feel wonderful, and the hassle of the previous week now seemed worth it.

She was brought back into reality when Beau passed a scribbled note to her. It simply said: *Do you think Mel is all right?* Parker shrugged her shoulders at Beau and felt a little guilty; she hadn't even thought about Mel. *Am I becoming so caught up in my own dramas that I'm becoming a selfish friend?*

Parker looked out the window; Amy had finished and was slinking back to her seat to the sound of thunderous applause led by Grayson, who was almost crying with laughter. An annoyed Ms Power commanded a performance from him, and Grayson was straight up from his seat, ready to perform his best Romeo. Grayson started to rap his monologue, full of all the bravado he was known for.

The other students laughed. Ms Power started to yell, and Parker was still lost in her thoughts looking out the window at the staff car park.

From out of nowhere, Parker saw a large dark-blue

lightning bolt shoot through the air and directly hit a car — Mr Baxter's beautiful brand-new car. The car he had just put himself into considerable debt to buy and had only owned for a week. This car still looked like it had just come off the production line. But it was now in flames in the car park, and Parker was floored. She knew the look of that lightning bolt — it may have been a darker blue than the one she produced with Griffin and Madison, but there was no mistaking the bolt.

Suddenly, Madison could feel people pushing past her. Her class were on their feet, all trying to get the best vantage point to see Mr Baxter's car burn. Comments were thick and fast, and laughter rang through the air. And then with a huge bang, the fuel tank on the car ruptured and the body of the car exploded, just as Mr Baxter ran outside. He was almost thrown back by the force of the explosion — instead, he fell to his knees. He was devastated his prized possession was now engulfed by flames and was a complete write off.

The entire class was standing at the windows, looking around the school; it seemed the entire school was looking out of windows at the burning car and the now-shattered Vice Principal.

All except for Parker, Madison and Griffin, who all remained seated, frozen to their seats. Only Parker saw the lightning, but the other two saw the dark-blue light that initially emitted from the blaze. Grayson, still roaring with laughter, called for Madison to come look, but noticed she was switching her attention from Griffin to Parker.

The three were stunned — could someone else share the same power as them?

That was when Parker turned her attention to Ms Power, the only other person not watching the inferno. Instead, she was watching the three students stare at each other, and she wanted answers.

CHAPTER ELEVEN: PARKER, MADISON & GRIFFIN

The school was in chaos. The alarm was still ringing, fire engines were multiplying by the minute, and children were everywhere. The school was known for its regular fire drills, and the students had rehearsed with precision their march to the sports oval, but today was different.

With an actual fire, mayhem ensued. When the alarm sounded, most students rushed to the staff car park — some to see the fire, some to see a devastated Mr Baxter, most to see both. Now that news cameras had arrived, the mayhem was amplified.

The fire engines had put out the fire, but the police were determined to get to the bottom of the explosion. They could not immediately understand how such an all-encompassing fire could start so quickly, and they certainly suspected that a teacher's car would probably only burn with the assistance of disgruntled students. Parents — who heard of the commotion from radio reports, calls and messages from their children — were now arriving and adding to the confusion. Plus, the media were trying to talk to any students they could find. It was complete pandemonium.

Parker and Beau headed straight for the oval; she was looking around for Madison and Griffin but couldn't see them. She needed to talk but didn't know how that would happen, due to all the chaos. She was close to telling Beau again of her 'powers', but there were so many people within ear shot that a private conversation between the pair would be heard by scores of others. Maybe Madison and Griffin were waiting for her in the staff toilet; it seemed the only place they all knew that was private. But she couldn't exactly leave Beau. He didn't like the other kids in school on the best of days, but today he looked plain scared of the mayhem.

Whenever the school captain, Xavier Gouskos, walked past, eyes followed. But unlike Madison, everyone liked Xavier, even the female teachers seemed to go a little coy when he was around. He was eighteen, had a chiselled jaw, thick dark hair and a defined body. He was often called 'The Greek God'. A sea of students parted as he walked through, all conversations ceasing. And surprisingly, he seemed to be walking straight to Parker and Beau. As he approached, he smiled showing his perfect teeth, and even Parker couldn't help but smile back.

'Hi, Beau, how are you?'

Beau grinned sheepishly, and Parker was shocked. She doubted Xavier knew her name, but he seemed to know Beau's. Beau stammered out a small answer, and Parker suddenly realised who Beau's secret crush was: the same as most of the girls in the school.

'Everything's going crazy around here, and the principal's asked me to round up some students to help get everyone back to some form of normality,' said the charming Xavier.

As if he will agree, thought Parker. Beau hated bringing attention to himself as much as she did, so there was no way he was going to drag blokey boys away from a car wreck.

'Sure, do I just come with you?'

Parker was floored, and Xavier answered in the positive.

Beau gave Xavier another goofy grin and turned to Parker. 'Did you want to help out?'

Parker could hardly believe what was happening to her best friend, but she liked it; he seemed happy. She would have loved to have seen him follow Xavier around like a little puppy, but this was the perfect escape for her to go and find Madison and Griffin. 'You go ahead,' she replied, before whispering, 'I mean, I wouldn't want to cramp your style.'

Beau quickly looked across to Xavier to see if he'd heard, but he was already deflecting unwanted advances from an overly made-up Year 11 girl. Beau smiled at Parker, pleased she'd guessed — it saved him the uncomfortable conversation he knew was overdue.

Xavier called for Beau to follow, and before Parker could say goodbye, Beau had disappeared into the crowd with a decidedly happier spring in his step.

Parker quickly turned the opposite way and tried to make her way out from the sports oval. The crowd was thick and didn't part as easy for her as they did for the school captain. Finally, after being abused several times, Parker got through the crowd of students. She walked to the staff toilets and could see the car park. She looked carefully through the chaos to find Madison. There were police and firemen everywhere. There were also news crews trying to bust through the police tape, and a small bunch of students who refused to move. Parker spotted Grayson being interviewed by a TV reporter, but no Madison — hopefully she was waiting somewhere for Parker.

Parker received some small resistance when she tried to re-enter the school. A bored Mr Anderson was half-standing guard at the front of the building. He had his phone out, and

Parker could tell he was quickly closing his Instagram as she approached. He made a small effort to stop her, but once she mentioned she was helping Xavier, he mumbled something under his breath and continued to fiddle with his phone.

The hallways were freaky. It was the middle of the day, and the noise from outside was overwhelming, but there was not a soul in the building, just the ringing of the fire alarm. Parker didn't like being alone in the huge corridors and hurried to the second level and hopefully the discussion she was dying to have.

She reached the staff toilet door and found it engaged. Was a teacher inside, some other students, or was that the meeting she wanted to attend? She knew there was no time for hesitation and softly tapped on the wooden door. A young male nervously asked who was there, and Parker knew it was Griffin. She answered with her name, and the door was suddenly flung open.

An impatient Madison stood with her hands on her hips and attitude splashed across her face. 'About time you got here.'

Soon, Parker was locked inside the small staff toilet, the scorch mark still proudly displayed on the roof. Somehow, she felt the safest she had since the incident with Baldy's car. She tried to explain what took her so long and how she couldn't just dump her best friend and come running into a restricted building.

'Why not? I told Amy to wait for me by the girls' toilet, she'll be there when I get back.'

Griffin was anxious to start talking about the fire; he didn't have friends to conveniently leave, so he had spent the past half an hour frantically waiting to talk to the girls. 'So, what happened? We all saw that blue light, right? Just like ours, only darker.'

But before the girls could answer, there was a loud and ferocious knock on the door. The three jumped, and Madison dropped the lip gloss she had been applying. The gloss landed on the new shoes she'd only just talked her father into buying her the week before, just after the robbery. It left a small stain, and Madison was furious. She wanted to scream and curse, but she stood frozen, as did Parker and Griffin.

All three held their breaths; they seemed afraid to make any noise.

The knocking continued, this time even more determined.

The three could see the door shake.

Suddenly, a familiar voice asked who was in the toilet — it was Ms Power, their English teacher.

Parker and Griffin turned to Madison with panic in their eyes — she was the best at making up plausible excuses, and Madison knew it. She readied her best 'ill' voice, the one reserved for her mother when she hadn't finished her history homework, and began her tall tale. 'I'm sorry, Ms, you're best to stick clear. I've been sick everywhere. It's green, it's chunky, and I think I may be contagious.' Madison smiled, and while slightly disgusted, the other two were impressed with how fast she could think on her feet.

But Tina was having none of it. 'Madison O'Sullivan, open this door right now.'

Madison and Parker shared a concerned glance — how did she know who was in the toilet?

A brief panic fell over Madison, the school was going through Armageddon, and she was about to be busted in a staff toilet with the two biggest dweebs in the school.

'I can't do that, Ms, I can barely move, and if we were in America, I'd suggest we call in the CDC. What's the Australian version, Ms?'

'Parker Bennett and Griffin Yates, the pair of you will be on detention for a full month unless you open this door immediately.'

She knew — Ms Power knew who was locked in the bathroom. All three immediately wondered exactly what she knew. Panic was well and truly setting in.

Griffin slowly unlocked the door, and before he could pull it open, Tina pushed her way into the now claustrophobic toilet. Tina's face was red from exertion, and the teens thought she was ready to explode.

'So now I guess I know how the scorch marks mysteriously appeared on the roof of THIS toilet.'

Parker was ready to cry. University was going to be hard enough to get into without a possible suspension for damaging school property. 'We weren't smoking in here. We wouldn't … I wouldn't.'

But Madison quickly interjected; she was okay with being busted for smoking, even though she detested cancer sticks. 'No, Ms, the three of us were in here smoking up a treat. Parker is like a smoking machine; she can even do smoke rings.'

Parker was floored, this was her nightmare, while Griffin just hoped that something, anything, would get them out of trouble.

'Really, Madison,' began Tina, 'was that before or after you were struck down with a contagious disease?'

Madison was quiet for the moment.

'I know what you've been doing in here. When I saw that car explode, I remembered, I finally remembered what happened in that shop and just exactly what you two did.'

The girls turned to each other — this was not good.

CHAPTER TWELVE:
TINA & THE TEENS

The fire alarm was finally shut off and the action had now died down. The shell of the car was on the back of a tow truck and being carted off. Most of the students returned to the oval, and the police had gotten rid of the news crews. Normality was slowly returning, and the teachers were trying to figure out how they could teach their lessons for the rest of the afternoon without more disruption.

All except for Mr Baxter, who barricaded himself in his office. The school's reception staff were sure they could hear him sobbing; this made them smile. Even they didn't like him.

Another notable exception was Tina, who was behind closed doors in her English room, where she had dragged a worried Parker, Madison and Griffin. They had been sitting there for five minutes and no one had said anything, even Madison was lost for words, and that was rare. The three wondered what Ms Power was thinking and what she thought she knew. She finally began to speak after what seemed like an eternity.

'I don't believe in a lot of things,' Tina started slowly. 'I don't believe in UFOs, and I don't believe in ghosts. I'm always the sceptic in my group of friends, but for the first time ever, I believe in magic.'

The three were confused; Ms Power was not one of those teachers that ever talked about themselves. They knew she had a small child, and that was all they knew, and here she was opening up ... opening up about their powers.

'Things happened so fast in that shop, and I was terrified, absolutely terrified. When he fired that gun, I thought I was going to die, and I blacked out. Next thing I knew, there were police everywhere, kids screaming and that awful smell from the fire. I had no idea what happened.'

Madison wished her amnesia was permanent; she was scared to hear what Ms Power had seen that day. Parker was enthralled by the tale; she just hoped it had an ending she liked. While Griffin was simply lost; he didn't know what to think.

'The doctors said it wasn't unusual. Your brain protects itself after a traumatic experience, and if I was going to remember what happened that day of the robbery, it would come back naturally. And I was okay with that, because I didn't know if I even wanted to remember. But then when that car exploded, it was that smell. The fire had a distinct smell I remembered from the robbery. And then I saw the three of you looking at each other. Everyone was panicked, excited and wondering what was happening, but not you three. And then it came flooding back ... every last detail.'

'You could have hallucinated, Ms, it's common in those kinds of situations,' Madison quickly added. She didn't want another person discovering their secret; this was starting to get out of control.

'Enough, Madison, I know. I know that you and Parker touched, and electricity came from your hands.'

The past few years had been rough for Tina. She'd moved

from her small country town of Peak Hill to attend university. She was worried she'd know no one and spend three years alone. But her neighbour in the university dorms, Natalie, soon became her best friend. They were both studying teaching and barely spent a moment apart. Tina soon met a wonderful guy, Aaron, an agriculture student. She fell in love and the three of them became an unbeatable team.

It was close to graduation and Tina took one last trip home; her parents were selling their property and Tina had to pack up a bedroom she never planned on living in again. The following year she was moving to Sydney with Aaron, with plans to live the life she always dreamed. It was on that trip home that Tina discovered she was carrying Aaron's child. She was over the moon and couldn't wait to tell him the good news. She rushed back to the campus and into Aaron's room — she never knocked, she never needed to. Not until that day.

Aaron jumped up, hurriedly piling on his clothes while Natalie tried to hide under the mess of bed sheets and covers. Tina was devastated, and no matter how hard Aaron and Natalie tried, she refused to talk to either. Then when she graduated, Tina calmly packed all her belongings into her old beat-up car and drove the 500 kilometres to Sydney.

She never told Aaron about his son, and she gave birth to him alone. Over time, she slowly began to make friends in Sydney, but she felt she could never really trust anyone. She often thought that if she didn't have her son, she would fall apart. She struggled and fought. Since the baby, she was worried she had put on too much weight. She didn't feel attractive, and her wage barely paid for her rent, food and childcare. She hated that her hair desperately needed a hairdresser, but she just couldn't afford to go. She had fought through postpartum depression and was finally ready to turn her life around, and then she entered that store. It had changed everything.

'You obviously didn't know what you were seeing, Ms, or maybe you've been abusing your medication. Does the school know you could be a whacko?' Madison was desperately trying to convince Ms Power she'd seen nothing, but even she knew it was futile.

'So now what?' was all Parker asked.

Tina hadn't actually thought that far ahead. Since the fire and the return of her memory, she was so focused on finding the three students, she hadn't thought what she was going to do with them. When the fire alarm had sounded, students had started pouring out of the classroom. She called out to Parker, but the sound of the alarm and the voices of all the students racing through the halls drowned out her voice. She started looking for them, but it was so crazy she could barely move through the student population. Finally, she'd seen Parker sneak back into the building, and followed her. When she saw the locked staff toilet, she knew her search was complete.

'So, are you gonna sell us out, Ms?' Madison's question shook Tina from her thoughts.

It was quiet for at least a minute, and the three teens were looking at each other, not sure if they should speak.

'No, of course not. I don't think you should tell anyone about it. How could they possibly understand?'

With the prompting of Tina, the three students began to explain all that had happened. All three, even Madison, felt a huge relief to be able to finally tell an adult. Secrets burn inside of you, and even though they had each other, it was good to talk to someone who didn't share the shame, and also get an outsider's perspective.

Tina listened — this was the most responsive students

had ever been to her. For the first time since she held her son, she felt a part of something important. She enjoyed being a part of their secret and knew she would do anything to help protect them.

'You can trust me, kids, I'll keep your secret. Anytime you need something, I'll help, because I think you'll need it.'

They knew she was right. If someone else shared the same abilities as them and had burnt a car, they may need her help.

CHAPTER THIRTEEN:
BRUCE

Parker floated through the afternoon. Classes resumed, but no one seemed ready to learn. Horrible rumours started that Mr Baxter had killed himself in his office, and the story only seemed to get worse and more creative as it spread from student to student. Not even the bellowing of Mrs Ling could stop the constant chatter in class. Grayson was bragging about his moment of fame on the news. Madison smiled and encouraged her boyfriend, but she kept stealing glances across to Griffin and Parker. Parker just stared into the distance; she couldn't comprehend any of this?

On the way home from school, Mel was still missing. Beau sent her a text to see if everything was fine, and she'd responded that everything was forgotten with the explosion, and she'd gone home early with a headache. Beau was excited to tell Parker all about his experiences as Xavier's shadow. He didn't have to do much, because whenever Xavier asked someone to do something, they would comply immediately. Parker couldn't remember Beau being so excited before; he told her about brushing hands with Xavier and how he knew nothing would ever happen. But it didn't stop him falling for him.

Moments after Beau and Parker hugged in front of his

house and she started the small walk back to her place, she received a text message. It was from a number she didn't know, but it said to go to Griffin's. She'd only recently saved his number to her phone, so it couldn't be him. She called the number, but it simply went to a message saying the phone was off. Parker was intrigued, though slightly concerned; did someone else in their school share her ability? She had never met Madison or Griffin at their houses; this seemed strange, especially in daylight. *Could this be a trap?*

Parker took her phone back out from her bag, she knew she was forbidden from phoning Madison unless this was an emergency, but this certainly seemed like an emergency. Nervously she found Madison's codename in her contacts and dialled. Madison had insisted on codenames. If one of her friends were going through her contacts, she couldn't be seen to have the numbers of her 'electricity pals' — that would be social suicide. So, she had chosen the names and insisted that those names be put in all their phones. She had watched as they did it, just to make sure.

For herself she had chosen Gigi. Partially because she thought she looked like Gigi Hadid, and partially after the classic movie that she and her grandparents loved to watch. She said they were all about elegance, and it was a natural fit. For Parker she chose Robin. She said that Batman had an annoying sidekick, so Parker would be her Robin. And her choice for Griffin was simple: Token. After all, he was the token male in the group. No objections would be heard, and like it or not, these were now their codenames.

The phone only rang once before Madison's picked up the call.

'What did I tell you about phoning me? Anyone could be around.'

Parker was full of apologises in her voice. 'I'm sorry, but

I got this text, and I don't know who it's from. I was worried it could have been those people who blew up Baxter's car.'

'It was me. If you're supposed to be one of the best minds in our school, then we are all doomed. Now hurry and get to Griffin's, I'm hiding in his back shed till you get here.'

And with that Madison was gone and Parker did what she was told, she headed to Griffin's, watching over her shoulder the whole way, making sure she wasn't being followed. Not because she was ashamed to go to Griffin's, quite the opposite, she was excited to be getting to know him finally. He was not the person she had originally thought, and she was pleased to be wrong. Instead, she was mindful of the fire starters from earlier that day. They could be anyone, and if they were setting Mr Baxter's car on fire, they were not people she wanted to know.

Parker cautiously stepped into the backyard and before she could look for the shed, she heard Madison call out to her in a hushed voice. 'Did you take the long way here?'

Griffin smiled as he came out from the shed, adjusting his eyes to the sunshine. Madison followed, still cautiously looking for signs of others. They entered the back door of Griffin's house. Parker realised Griffin's family didn't have as much money as hers. Her family struggled at times, but it was nothing compared to what she imagined Griffin's family went through. The furniture was old, and nothing in the house looked remotely new. Instead of the slick interiors of many places, this home was filled with loads of photos and small trinkets. It was a house filled with love. Parker immediately felt at ease and smiled at Griffin; he smiled back, his embarrassment easing.

In the corner of the family room sat a TV broadcasting news headlines for the day. All three stopped when they saw their school featured as the story of the day. Familiar faces were rushing past in a quick montage, and then they showed a snippet of one student being interviewed, naturally it was Grayson.

'Everyone here is just really shocked; this is not the kind of thing you expect at such a good school like this.'

Parker and Griffin looked at each other and rolled their eyes, while Madison beamed with pride — she was so proud that out of everyone in the school, they had chosen her boyfriend to interview, although it didn't surprise her.

'Look at him, isn't he just so hot?'

Parker and Griffin didn't respond, they didn't need to. The next news item was about another fire-bombing attack on an ATM in the local area, the third in a short amount of time. Police were still baffled as to how the attacks were taking place, and just who the culprits might be. The three didn't hear the story, they were instead focused on the voice coming from inside the house.

'Is that you, Grif?' called out a male voice, who the girls assumed was his dad.

Madison looked panicked. Griffin calmly walked across to the other side of the family room and opened his bedroom door. He ushered the girls in, and then he answered back to his father that he had just gotten home.

'Your school was all over the news. I looked for you in the footage but couldn't see you.'

Griffin told the girls he'd be back in a few minutes and closed the door behind them. Griffin's room was a film geek's dream. There was barely any wall visible with all the film posters that lined the space. Most were from dark films and films with a supernatural edge — pride of place were the posters of *Silence of the Lambs* and *The Sixth Sense*. On top of his bookcase sat some movie action figures, all in boxes and in pristine condition.

'Cute, he collects dolls.' Madison chuckled at Griffin's expense.

Meanwhile, Parker was impressed with his commitment to collecting.

Griffin finally re-entered after a few minutes, saying he'd told his dad he needed to study, and they were free to talk. Griffin was keen to know why Madison chose his place for the meeting.

'Simple, I have people at my house, and Parker has a little brother who can tell anyone about who she was entertaining,' returned Madison. The truth was, of course, that she could have easily snuck in Parker and Griffin, but today was not a good day at home. Lachlan had taken a turn for the worse, and there was a constant stream of medical staff in and out of her house — she didn't want her new friends to ask any personal questions.

Madison quickly moved on, pretending she wanted to get out of there to see Grayson. She really wanted to go see her brother, fearing he may not make it through the week. She produced two brand new mobile phone boxes and handed them to a surprised Parker and Griffin.

'Amy was trying to get a number out of my phone this morning and asked who Token was, so I had to make up some story. We now have our own pre-paid phones. Keep them charged and on you at all times, but make sure they're on silent. No actual calls, just text messages, it's the safest way to communicate and not get caught. Someone else out there has the same ability as us and they're not being careful. Today's attack on Baldy's car may have been amusing, but it was stupid and an easy way to get the wrong kind of attention.'

'Ms Power said she'd let us know any info she hears off the other teachers,' added Parker; she was starting to enjoy the espionage intrigue.

'Good, and we all travel in different circles, so let's keep it that way. See if you can find out any info. We need to work out who these people are before they find us,' concluded Madison. She always saw herself as a leader, and today was no different. 'And one more thing. We need practise, just in case we have to use our power again. It's way too unpredictable now.'

The other two agreed — neither wanted to use their power against anyone, but they all had a feeling this was probably going to come to a head. They all took out their phones and agreed to meet at the park at 9pm that night. They were ready to leave when suddenly Griffin's door flung open and there was Griffin's dad, Bruce.

Madison looked for somewhere to dive, but it was too late to hide, while Parker and Griffin had very guilty looks on their faces.

Bruce smiled; he knew he had burst in on something. 'So, what's going on in here mate?'

Bruce, like his father before him, was a builder. Even his mother was an ace with a hammer and nails. The accident happened not long after the happiest moment of his life. His son was born, and he felt untouchable. Griffin had been suffering from a particularly nasty case of colic, and sleep hadn't been easy for the entire family. But Bruce didn't really mind; fatherhood had been his dream for such a long time. Maybe it was the lack of sleep, maybe it was the focus on telling the guys on the site about the wonders of his son, or maybe it really was just a tragic accident, but Bruce had fallen from the roof of a two-storey house he'd been building and landed on a pile of timber. His back was broken, and he was left permanently in a wheelchair.

'Thanks for the help with that assignment, Griffin, we better be off to do some more research. The school almost burns down, and they still find time to pile on the assignments.' Madison tried her usual excuse routine, but Bruce just smiled again. It had been so long since he'd seen his son bring friends home that this moment brought him joy.

'So, is one of these young ladies the girl you keep talking about?' added Bruce, enjoying the lovely shade of red that Griffin's face had turned.

Griffin took a step towards the door, ready to show the girls out, but he knew his dad had purposely parked his wheelchair in the door frame, blocking any exit.

'I'm Parker, and this is Madison'.

Madison smiled, not quite understanding why real names had to be used at this point.

Bruce smiled wider and said hello. He could see Griffin getting more embarrassed and he knew the girl that Griffin liked was in the room.

'Well, I better let you ladies get home, but please feel free to visit any time. I know Grif would really love that.' Bruce could feel daggers being shot from his son's eyes, so he took his time wheeling out of the door frame, just to drag the moment on. He didn't get much of a chance to rib his son in front of company, and he was going to relish it.

The girls thanked Bruce and then left, with Madison reminding them all about doing their practical later that night.

When the girls had gone, Bruce started asking his son questions, none of which were answered. He laughed as he was left talking to his son's bedroom door. He had noticed a change in Griffin lately, a good change, and he thought he knew why: love.

CHAPTER FOURTEEN:
AMIE & MEL

Parker, Madison and Griffin met at the park that night and managed not to set any trees alight. They practised their art for an hour and managed to start controlling the electricity fields. They all felt a strong sense of pride, and the connection that was building between them only seemed to be making the lightning bolt stronger.

Griffin suggested they try and channel their power into hitting a fifty-cent coin right across the other side of the park. They were all keen to see if they could control the power that specifically until Madison's phone rang. It was Grayson; it had been a big day for him with his appearance on the news, and he'd been fielding phone calls from his friends all night. He was getting ready for bed and wanted his nightly phone call with Madison.

She signalled to the others that she was leaving, and left, without saying goodbye. And then she listened as Grayson bragged about his fifteen minutes of fame and whether he should try and get an agent.

The practice was over, and Parker and Griffin slowly left, proud of their achievements. Griffin walked Parker the short distance home, but on the way, Beau called and still wanted to talk about his adventure with Xavier. Griffin proceeded to walk home alone; his phone stayed silent.

It was lucky that the trio had left when they did ...

Only minutes after they had turned off the street, the sound of two brand-new trail bikes was heard roaring into the cul-de-sac. It was the Thomas twins. They'd been burning through cash, spending up big on all the things they'd always dreamt of owning.

They were smiling as they were riding, tearing into the park, skidding to a halt, and ripping up the grass. The pair jumped off their bikes, having the time of their lives. They hardly noticed the girls arrive; they were too busy talking about the feeling of riding the bikes. But when they saw Aime and Mel, they greeted them with kisses, and again dark-blue light floated around them as their lips connected.

The boys didn't think they needed to practise anymore — they were professionals, and nothing could stop them now. They were already trying to think of ways they could improve their wealth with bigger and better crimes; they just needed to think of them. An armoured truck maybe?

The girls looked at each other, sharing the same thought. Even when they walked to meet the boys, they walked together. There was something about this ability that was making them understand each other more, it just seemed the twins were closing their minds to the girls and were only worried about each other.

Amie was the first to mention it; she shocked Mel when she showed up to walk with her. Mel knew Amie had something to get off her chest.

'The thing is, I think I might love Arlo, and I'm happy to go along with what he wants.'

Mel agreed, as she felt the same about Devon. 'But the problem is they seem to be a little sloppy and just a little overconfident.'

Both the girls had big dreams for the future. Mel wanted to go to university and study molecular biology, while Amie was desperate to become a buyer for a major retailer. Both knew a police record would make these dreams impossible. There were times they felt invincible when they could see, and even more so feel the electricity shoot from their hands. But no matter how powerful they felt, if arrested, no secret power was stopping them from a jail cell.

Then there were the boys' new reckless spending habits. In the past few days, the boys had splurged big time with the cash they stole from three different ATMs. There were the trail bikes, the new widescreen flat TV, as well as the latest gaming consoles, and the games to match.

The girls knew this was only the first dip in the ocean.

So, they agreed they needed to speak to the boys, and Amie decided Mel should be the one to broach the topic with the boys. Mel was not good at refusals and had agreed but knew she would regret it.

The twins were staring at their bikes, encouraging the girls to look closely at how amazing their new toys were. Amie looked at Mel — it was now time to talk to the boys.

Mel took a deep breath and readied herself, this could end badly. 'Do we think it's the best idea to flaunt our new-found cash?'

Amie watched on nervously. If the boys turned against Mel, she'd play dumb.

Arlo asked why not; his question contained at least two swear words.

'It's just that if they start looking for people who could have committed the robberies, wouldn't they start looking for people spending a lot of cash?' Mel braced herself for a tirade of words, or even worse, violence. She was surprised when instead she was greeted by a large smile from Devon.

He reached inside his pocket, returning with a closed fist, lifting it slowly towards Mel. 'So does that mean that you don't want this?' Devon opened his fist to reveal an amazing diamond-encrusted bracelet that seemed to sparkle under the moonlight. Devon's smile seemed to match the glitter of the jewellery.

Mel's breath was taken away; she never expected a boy to ever buy her something so glorious, even if it was from the proceeds of crime. 'That is the most amazing thing I have ever seen in my life! But ... where would I wear it without a million questions about where it came from?'

Amie was surprised Mel had such strength, and tenacity — she wouldn't be so bold. But then she was called on to speak her mind by Arlo. He wanted to know if she agreed; the question was asked while she was being presented with a ridiculously expensive designer watch. Arlo knew Amie was all about the brand names.

Amie stood silent for at least two minutes; Arlo was ready to ask the question again before Amie carefully chose her words. 'It's not that I agree with her,' her delivery was slow, 'it's just that she might be right. The cops will be on the lookout for people spending recklessly.'

The boys should have been angry, and usually they would have flown off the handle if someone dared to question them. But the girls were a part of them now, and more importantly, they couldn't continue to terrorise the city without the help of their accomplices.

The twins carefully considered what the girls had said, and agreed, to an extent. What use was money if you couldn't spend it? So, the boys agreed to cut down on their extravagant spending, plus they had their bikes now. The boys wanted to celebrate the agreement with more cash. The jewellery for the girls had been expensive, and they couldn't stop now, they were having too much fun.

That night, they blew up another ATM, more skilfully this time. There was less mess, less effort in pulling apart the machine, and they were faster. They felt like they'd perfected the art of destroying cash machines, soon they would need a bigger challenge. They needed to up the ante and were more than ready.

CHAPTER FIFTEEN:
THE NEW KID

The English room seemed a strange place to Parker now, with everything turned on its head. Before, she'd only speak to Beau and Mel and was left alone by everyone else, she even thought Ms Power never liked her much. But now she was getting constant glances from Madison and Griffin.

Ms Power was encouraging her opinion in class, praising her work, and smiling at her constantly. Worst of all, Mel had started to become distant. She never wanted to hang around with her and Beau anymore; some lunch breaks she just wouldn't show up to their bench. Parker wondered if it was because she hadn't been a very good friend lately and spent enough time with Mel.

Ms Power was giving back the essays the class had written about *Romeo and Juliet*. Tina smiled as she gave Parker hers: written in red writing on the top was Top Mark. Parker knew she deserved her score, she loved Shakespeare, and English had always been her best subject. But she also worried her new friendship with Ms Power may be influencing her marks. Parker tried to hide her paper, but Beau had already spotted her mark and was loudly congratulating her. Parker was embarrassed and worried about what Madison and Griffin would think.

Parker just wanted to get on with the lesson, she knew they were ready to start a Jane Austen novel today, and she was itching to get back into some work. First, Ms Power wanted the new student to stand in front of the class and introduce himself. Parker thought it was strange that a new student would be starting in the second half of the year. She never usually paid much attention to the boys in school, but there was something striking about this new boy. She stared at him as he nervously walked to the front of the class. He had sandy blonde hair, golden tanned skin and piercing blue eyes, and Parker couldn't believe how attracted she immediately felt to him.

The girls in the class were all whispering about him; Amy seemed particularly keen. Grayson and Henry saw the attention that the new boy was getting and instantly took a dislike to him.

He squirmed as the entire room of eyes watched his every move, and he stammered as he spoke. 'Hi, my name is Kyle, and I've just moved here from Adelaide.'

After the incident with his mother and Shane, Kyle knew things had to change. Only days after the incident in which Shane was left hospitalised, his mum returned to Shane's bedside. She paid for an electrician to check for faults in the house, figuring it must have been an electrical problem that caused the accident that hurt Shane. She told Kyle he'd have to get the house ready for Shane's return home. Kyle found a new strength and offered his mother a simple choice — either him or Shane.

Shortly after, Kyle was moving to Sydney to live with his grandmother. She'd wanted him to come live with her since Shane entered their life, and Kyle was glad to come to Sydney. To the same suburb as the girl that appeared on the cover of the newspaper that helped him shoot an amazing bolt of electricity through his house, straight at Shane.

After mumbling a few pieces about himself, Kyle slid back into his seat. He noticed that most of the girls suddenly losing interest in him. Kyle didn't mind, why should his new school be any different? And plus, he only had eyes for one girl. He watched Parker the whole way back to his seat, turning his gaze momentarily when she would look at him. On several occasions, their eyes met, but embarrassed, both turned away.

At recess, Kyle went searching for Parker. He looked around most of the school, even facing a barrage of insults from Grayson and his cronies. It wasn't until just before the bell that he found his target.

There was Parker, holding court in between Beau and Mel. Kyle paused for a moment; this was completely out of character for him. Back in Adelaide, there was no way he would have walked up to a girl to introduce himself, but he knew Parker was no ordinary girl.

Parker was mid-sentence when she saw Kyle approaching. She stopped talking, and Beau seemed surprised, nothing could usually stop his best friend mid-story. Then he saw Kyle walking towards them and smiled; he was not the only one to have a crush. Parker, a little embarrassed, turned away, just as Mel was trying to hide her new bracelet under her school jacket. But the diamonds caught the sun and shined straight into Parker's eyes.

'Oh my God, Mel, where did you get that bracelet?'

Mel immediately tried to pull her sleeves down further, but it was too late. Parker, and now Beau, had seen her gift from Devon. With a red face, Mel tried to explain herself while stumbling. 'Well, the thing is, it's my mum's, and she doesn't know I'm wearing it, so please don't tell her.'

Parker and Beau looked at each other — this was strange. Beau asked why she would do that and why she would bring something so valuable to school?

Mel was getting quite frazzled and was keen for a distraction. 'Why do you think the new kid is coming over here?'

And before the pair could answer, Kyle was there, full of nervous smiles.

'I don't know anybody, so do you mind if I sit with you?'

Parker wanted to answer straight away, but for some reason the words wouldn't come out. She didn't quite understand what was happening; she was never like this in front of boys, but then again, she'd never been immediately captivated by a boy before.

'Of course you can sit with us. I'm Beau.' Beau warmly extended his hand, and Kyle felt some relief. Mel followed suit, though not as eagerly, and then the small group turned to Parker, whose face was now a deep shade of red.

She gently placed out her hand, and Kyle held his breath as they touched for the first time. He expected sparks, another lightning bolt, but instead all he got was a stammered introduction from Parker. He was slightly disappointed there weren't fireworks when they first touched, but he would not give up this quickly. He'd travelled so far to meet her, and plus, he couldn't think of any other explanation as to why her photo had stopped the person he hated most in this world. He knew Parker had helped him — he just didn't know how.

Beau chuckled to himself when he realised how quiet Parker was.

There were so many things Parker wanted to ask and say, but every time she went to speak, no voice came out. She couldn't understand what was happening.

Beau instead filled the silence, asking Kyle all kinds of questions, things he thought Parker would want to know. In between the questions, he fed Kyle with lots of interesting facts about Parker.

Mel was at first unsure what was happening, but mid-conversation she received a text message from Devon demanding her presence, and she spent the rest of the time trying to find excuses to leave.

Kyle sat relieved and content. As soon as he had entered the English classroom, he could see Parker and her pals were on the outer, a fringe-dwelling group in the school's popularity contest. This eased his mind, as he was worried she may have been one of the popular girls. He knew she was pretty enough. He just hoped he might finally make some friends, some good friends.

The bell rang, bags and folders were collected. Kyle asked where Mrs Ling's History room was, and Beau smiled.

'Parker's in that class, she can take you, and you can sit with her. We know how hard it must be on your first day.'

Kyle smiled; Parker half-smiled. This is what she truly wanted, but part of her felt the urge to vomit, to literally bend over and just vomit. As Parker and Kyle headed for the classroom, Parker was finally able to string a coherent sentence together.

Griffin saw them. He looked at the pair walking closely, talking, laughing, and he exhaled slowly. This made him unhappy.

CHAPTER SIXTEEN: PARKER & KYLE

Parker finally overcame her initial nerves and was loving spending time with Kyle. The whole way to class they chatted. Mrs Ling had to bellow at her three times to be quiet, and it wasn't till she was threatened with detention that Parker fell silent.

Madison couldn't help but smile as she saw Parker delicately place her hair behind her ear as she talked to the new boy. She could see the instant spark between the pair and was surprised she was happy for her secret friend. However, Griffin, who sat alone at the side of the classroom, looked on scowling. He was not happy at all with the arrival of this new boy.

By the time Beau had arrived at their usual meeting point for lunch, Parker was already sitting with Kyle, both laughing. Beau was delighted. He walked straight across and was greeted by a huge smile from Parker. He asked about Mel, and Parker relayed the bizarre message from Mel that she had returned home at lunch, her mum busting her for wearing the expensive bracelet to school.

'Is it just me or is Mel acting really strange lately?' asked Beau. While Parker may have been his best friend, he still really cared for Mel. He loved how she laughed at all his jokes, even the bad ones, and she had always been a great listener.

Before Parker could answer, she spotted Griffin in her peripheral vision. She turned to see the brooding Griffin walking directly across to her. *If Madison sees this, she'll kill us both.'*

But as determined as he was on approach to Parker, he changed tact at the last minute and walked away.

Parker wondered what he was doing, especially so publicly.

Beau chuckled. 'Hey, Parker, looks like your stalker is back.'

'What?' stammered Parker; this was the first time Beau had mentioned anything like this. He'd never even talked about Griffin.

'Haven't you seen the way he looks at you in class? And I'm sure I saw him following us home last week. He has it bad for you.' Then Beau smiled as he prepared for his final statement; he knew it was going to cause uneasiness. 'We'll just have to tell him that you're not available now'.

Kyle almost choked on his sandwich, while Parker went a deep shade of red. Beau's smile was even bigger now; the only thing he enjoyed more than seeing his best friend happy, was seeing her flustered.

'Griffin's okay, and me, I'm still, I'm ... um.' For being the top of her English class, Parker was doing a terrible job of stringing together a simple sentence. 'What about Mel, hey? She's acting really weird.'

Parker's deflect didn't really work; Beau laughed out loud, unable to control his giggles.

Kyle got over his initial embarrassment. He was now focused on Griffin. Kyle was new to the dating scene, he'd never had a girlfriend; in fact, he was yet to experience his first kiss. He'd finally found the girl he wanted to share it with, but he never imagined there'd be someone else who'd be pursuing her too. He knew he would have to make a move soon, but he just didn't know how.

The bell rang, and Kyle was disappointed to learn he had no classes with Parker that afternoon. He would have even enjoyed some classes with Beau. Without his new friends, he figured he'd be sitting alone, like he did back in Adelaide.

As the three walked back to class, Beau came up with the perfect idea. 'So, Kyle, Parker and I are gonna hang out after school, wanna join us?'

It was now close to 3.30, and Parker impatiently waited for the doorbell to ring at her house. She found herself peering through the venetian blinds for her visitor. But as soon as she peered through them, she would immediately release them. She couldn't let Kyle see her waiting, she had to somehow try and be casual. Her brother began to ask her what she was doing. She told him she was waiting for Beau, but her mother thought it strange. She always locked herself in her room before Beau came over, which was most days. Why would she be so nervous about seeing him today?

Meanwhile, Kyle walked around the block so many times that old Frida near the park had the phone in her hand, ready to call the police if he passed her house one more time.

And still, Kyle arrived way too early, he didn't know the neighbourhood properly and hadn't wanted to be late. So, he arrived fifteen minutes early. He paced, continuously. He was so nervous that he hadn't even noticed that he was being followed, closely.

At exactly 3.30 the doorbell rang, and Parker ran to get it. She stopped, realising she may seem desperate if she opened the door within seconds of the bell. Her brother laughed at her, and her mum seemed unsure what to think. Parker centred herself, breathed deeply and casually opened the door. She smiled when she saw Kyle; he smiled back. And then Parker's mum smiled — it was now obvious why her daughter was acting so strangely.

Parker's breath was taken away slightly. Kyle was no longer in his uniform; instead, he wore a tight jumper that hugged his torso. Parker felt her eyes drawn to his arms but tried to focus on his eyes. Flustered again, she invited him in.

Parker's mum made the pair a quick snack; this was also an exercise in finding out who her daughter was so obviously besotted with.

Alistair spent a great deal of time wanting to be looked at. He was not popular at school, so when his sister brought friends home, he was like a little puppy bouncing up and down. Parker pleaded to her mother with her eyes. Mrs Bennett knew she shouldn't let her daughter head to her room with a boy, but she couldn't help but be caught up in the excitement. Plus, she trusted her daughter. So off they walked, full of smiles. It was only Alistair that was left upset; if he had a tail, it would have stopped wagging.

As soon as they entered her room, which she had hurriedly cleaned, they sat on the floor. She hoped he couldn't see under her bed; it was jam-packed with all the items that had been strewn across her room just a small time ago.

The pair sat close without touching, but there seemed to be a surge pulsing between them. They smiled; this was the first time they'd truly been alone. Kyle wasn't sure how to start the conversation; this was uncharted territory for him. He opened his mouth to speak, unsure what would pour out, when Parker's phone suddenly vibrated.

She smiled, slightly annoyed they were interrupted. She

apologised, picked up the phone and was surprised that the text was from Beau. He was late — he was *never* late.

> *Sorry, Park, can't make it this afternoon. I could make an excuse, but thought you'd like an afternoon alone with just you and the new kid. You better phone me when he leaves and tell me every single detail. Xxx.*

Parker made some excuse on behalf of Beau. She noticed a grin form on Kyle's face. This made Parker grin too.

'Thank you,' uttered Kyle through his grin.

Parker was confused and asked him why he was thanking her.

'This is my first day, and I already feel like I belong here. Back home ...' Kyle paused, and Parker leaned forward; she was enthralled. 'I hated that school. I went there every single day, for all those years, and no one bothered to take the time to get to know me.'

Parker knew how he felt, and at that moment she felt so thankful for Beau.

'And things at home weren't very good. I think somewhere along the line, my mum forgot that she actually had to be a mother.'

Parker was unsure about what to say. She was surprised Kyle had such a troubled past. She was suddenly thankful for the family she so often whined about. She wanted to hug him, she wanted to hold his hand, but most of all she wanted to kiss him. She reached forward to touch his hand, but before she could connect, she was distracted by the light illuminating from her phone. This wasn't the phone sitting next to her, but her secret phone that was silent and sitting on her desk. She leaned forward to see the screen; she'd received many messages, but never a call. That was when she saw the name, *Token*, flashing on her screen. *Why is Griffin calling?*

She knew she should answer, but in that moment, she didn't care about her power or the secret collection of misfits she'd formed. She was enthralled by Kyle and was hypnotised by the sound of his voice. She turned away from the phone and beamed at Kyle. 'I'm glad you're here.'

The conversation continued to flow.

Kyle told Parker about Shane and all his problems. He just failed to mention the incident that had led him to track down Parker. Parker opened up and told Kyle things she would usually only reserve for Beau. She mentioned her hopes, her dreams, but she omitted desires for the moment. They talked the superfluous as well: films and music. Some they had in common and others they enjoyed arguing about. When Parker listed *The Notebook* as one of her favourite films, Kyle groaned and paid her out. How could she be the intellectual she claimed to be and love that type of soap opera? Parker loved it, the challenge was exciting, and she smiled as she began to debate him.

They talked for a full hour, non-stop chatter.

Alistair stuck his head through the door once, but when one of Parker's shoes almost landed squarely on his nose, he didn't dare try to enter again.

Kyle had bided his time and was now desperate to ask a question about the incident that got her on the front cover of the national newspapers.

'You know, my grandma told me about what happened to you in your kitchen, and then I remembered the story on the front page of my paper back home. I read your article the night I decided that I wasn't going to put up with my mum's boyfriend anymore. You gave me strength.'

Parker turned red, even if he didn't once mention fry

pans. He mentioned her strength — no one ever talked about that. She briefly told him what happened. She just hoped he hadn't heard about the convenience store, because she wasn't sure how she'd explain that one. She'd been so honest that she was worried she'd just blurt out she was a witch and be okay if he wanted to burn her at the stake. Parker was staring deeply into Kyle's eyes. They were deep and intense but also rich with colour.

It was in that moment that they changed; Parker could see a determination in them.

'You're pretty incredible, Parker Bennett. I hope you know that.' The moment was right; Kyle closed his eyes and started to lean forward.

A small grin escaped from the side of Parker's mouth as she followed suit, closing her eyes and leaning forward. Parker was a romantic and always hoped her first kiss would be amazing, and this was going to be better than she could ever have imagined.

Parker could feel the warm breath of Kyle slowly approaching her when she was shaken from the moment by a tapping at her bedroom window. She instantly fell forward, missing Kyle's lips and falling onto his chest. Annoyed and slightly embarrassed, she opened her eyes and saw Griffin standing at her window, shock painted across his face. It was then she noticed the cloud of blue lightning that danced around her and Kyle. She was stunned, especially when she saw Kyle proudly smiling, unfazed.

CHAPTER SEVENTEEN: MRS BENNETT

Madison worried she wasn't spending enough time with her brother Lachlan. With time dedicated to her boyfriend, shopping trips, hangouts with Amy and Amie, and now her secret rendezvous with her self-described 'freaky friends', there was hardly time for Lachlan. The doctor had come to visit again this morning and the mood in the house was very sombre.

Madison loved playing video games with her brother, but he was too weak to play now. Instead, she would sit and watch TV, or read to him. She never read novels, neither of them wanted that. And she thought newspapers were too depressing. Rather, she kept a large supply of magazines next to his bed. Some were cars, some were surfing, but today she was reading to him from *Cosmopolitan*. It wasn't that he wanted to hear the latest in fashion or makeup tips, he just loved hearing his sister read, and she was more enthusiastic when she was reading subject matter that interested her personally.

Madison was in the middle of a particularly inspired story on dating tips for the modern women when she saw her secret phone glowing in her bag. At first, she ignored it, but then it glowed again. Two messages in the space of a minute. She apologised profusely to her brother and pulled her phone from her bag. She angrily opened the messages, one from the sender Robin, the other, Token. Both read the same: *Emergency, Robin's house.*

Madison threw the phone back in her tiny designer handbag, annoyed her time with Lachlan was interrupted. She continued to read, but she was missing words and repeating sentences.

Lachlan knew her mind was no longer focused on seven steps to survive the dating scene. 'If you need to go, that's okay. I've probably had enough Cosmo for today, anyway.'

'No, those people can wait; I'm here with you now, that's all that matters,' Madison said it with all her heart. Her mother had only just told her to prepare for the worst.

'It's obviously important, and I promise I won't die while you're gone.' Lachlan tried to laugh but ended up coughing.

Madison told him it wasn't funny, but he still thought it was. It took a few minutes, but Lachlan convinced Madison that it was okay for her to leave. He was tired anyway and wanted to sleep so he wouldn't drift off during *Ninja Warrior* that evening.

With a kiss on his forehead and an excuse to her parents, Madison was out the door. She text that she was on her way; it was a text in complete caps. She was angry, and she was ready to take it out on them. She was also angry at having to go to Parker's house. She'd never been inside, even though it was only two streets away. She looked around to make sure no one could see her ringing the bell and then impatiently waited. The minute it took for the door to open seemed like an eternity, especially for a girl petrified of losing her social standing.

Mrs Bennett was dumbfounded when she opened the

door to reveal Madison. She honestly expected it to be Beau, just like she did when Griffin had rung the door minutes before. And before she could even open her mouth, Parker instantly appeared behind her with Kyle and Griffin, trying to usher Madison hastily in her room.

'Hang on, what's going on around here today? And where's Beau?' Mrs Bennett asked.

All of them instantly looked guilty, especially Parker. It looked like she was going to be adding someone new to this group, and it wasn't Beau. She hated hiding things from him.

The boys were both unsure what to say. Griffin was still eyeing off Kyle, while Kyle himself still held onto the excitement of the electricity that had flowed between him and Parker.

Madison, however, was forming excuses; she would need to make up a story here, and fast. 'We were given this ridiculous group assignment, and we all got put into groups. Beau is currently doing his assignment with my boyfriend Grayson and my best friends, Amy and Amie. He SO got the best group.'

Parker got a vision of that group in her head, and she shuddered for poor Beau — even the mere thought terrified her.

Mrs Bennett wasn't as sure. Parker usually told her everything, and she was sure she would have mentioned being forced to work with Madison, a girl she didn't seem to like. 'And just what subject is this assignment for?'

Both Parker and Madison answered simultaneously. It was just a shame their answers were different.

Parker uttered, 'English', while Madison chimed in with 'History'. Guilt planted itself further on the faces of the teens.

'I didn't realise English and History did joint assignments, that seems rather odd, especially when Beau doesn't even do History, does he?' Parker's mum wasn't angry, just suspicious. Parker wasn't the typical teenager — was this all about the change? She searched their faces for an answer. Panic had started to set in, and Mrs Bennett knew it. She knew Madison's family. Madison may have had her moments, but Mrs Bennett still thought she was essentially a good kid. She did share that one terrifying moment with Parker, but she hadn't thought they'd spoken since that afternoon. Griffin was quiet, she knew that. And she knew his family. She was aware of the struggles he'd been through and was actually happy Parker had befriended him. But who was this new boy? And why did he look so familiar? 'Kyle, what is your last name?'

'You don't know him. He's just moved here, Mum, from Adelaide,' Parker quickly chimed in. She wanted to find a way out of this.

'That wasn't my question, and I'm sure Kyle can answer for himself.' Mrs Bennett rarely got to play the tough mother, and she had to admit she quite enjoyed it.

'It's Fuller, Kyle Fuller.'

'Is your mum Sharon? Her maiden name Drewitt, by any chance?' asked Mrs Bennett.

Kyle quickly answered yes.

'I thought you looked familiar. I went to school with your mum. I hadn't seen her for years, and then we ran into each other in hospital. We were sharing a hospital room after you two were born; only a day apart, you know? Please tell your mum that Julia says hi.'

Parker was floored — her mum knew Kyle's.

Kyle was also taken aback; he hadn't heard someone speak fondly about his mother in such a long time. He wanted to ask her so many questions. His mother hated talking about the past; she said her life started again after the divorce, but to Kyle that was when it all started going downhill.

Alistair had been standing and watching the group, he loved having this many people in his house and was desperate to be involved. 'Hey, Madison, is Lachlan going to a new school, cause I haven't seen him in ages?'

This was it for Madison, she wanted out of there now. It was bad enough she was pulled away from her dying brother, now she was being forced to speak to people she didn't want to.

'As lovely as all this is. I can't stay long. So, let's do this ...' She paused. 'This homework, so I can go and hang with my actual friends.' Done, no one would now be under the impression she wanted to be there.

Julia Bennett was satisfied for now. She was always going to let them run off and have their secret meeting. She knew at their age it couldn't be anything too important. So, she released the four to the safety of Parker's room; Alistair was again left disappointed.

Parker led her friends into her bedroom and asked Griffin to pass her a chair from behind her desk and barricaded the door so no one could just walk in.

'But won't your mum get angry if she sees you've locked her out?'

'It's not for her, it's for my brother.'

Madison was tired of idle chatter, she'd already been in this house for ten minutes, and that was about eleven minutes too long for her liking. 'Why did you call me over, and why is the new kid here? You better not have told him anything.'

Parker didn't need to answer Madison, she simply turned to Kyle. 'Think of something that makes you angry.'

This was simple for Kyle — he thought about Shane. He thought about his mother. He had phoned her once since arriving in Sydney, and she had made up an excuse to get off the phone, but Kyle could hear Shane in the background bellowing for her to hang up. She hadn't yet phoned him back, and Kyle doubted whether she ever would.

Parker could see pain flash in Kyle's deep eyes; she wanted to ask him if he was all right. She'd asked for him to be angry, but she didn't think this would cause him such pain and turmoil. However, she needed to concentrate, so she thought again of the sweaty criminal in the convenience store and how he made her feel. She reached across and touched Kyle's hand. Sparks charged from their joined hands, and electricity passed between the pair — a beautiful blue light danced lazily above them.

Kyle smiled at Parker, this was so unbelievable, but at the same time, it was everything he'd wanted.

Griffin was in shock, how was this kid able to share their power?

Parker was excited, she was happy to share this bond with the boy she liked.

Meanwhile, Madison was floored and unsure what to think.

'Well, Madison, did you want to know about this, or not?' asked Parker, and the four all stood speechless.

CHAPTER EIGHTEEN: ARLO

Mel hadn't returned to school after lunch earlier that day, neither had Amie. Excuses were made to friends, and the pair met up with Arlo and Devon. This was the first time the girls had been inside the Thomas house, and they were suitably underwhelmed. The house was a mess, and the smell of stale beer and slight aroma of dried urine was fighting for prominence. The old carpet was stained with patches of vomit, and the lounges were ripped.

Both girls were stepping slowly through the pile of empty beer bottles, careful not to step on anything. Neither knew what type of disease they could get. Even though the pair weren't the 'best' of friends, they stuck close, because in this ghetto all they had was each other.

It was a different story when they pushed open the door to the twin's room. The door was littered with safety locks and padlocks, and the words *Stay out, Dad* were proudly spray-painted across the pine door in thick, black, crudely painted letters. Inside the room lay a teenage boy's treasure trove. All the items the boys had proudly bragged about were crammed into the small bedroom. It seemed the boy's bunk beds were now an afterthought, pushed into the furthest corner of the room, surrounded by the most modern, and most expensive high-tech items. The focus of the room was no doubt the impressively large flat screen television, which seemed hideously inappropriate for a room that size.

The boys ushered the girls into their room. They were proud of their little paradise and were excited to let the girls be the first and only people to see and share in it. They kissed their girls, the dark-blue light emanating as they did. The boys were enjoying their suspension, especially when their dad spent most of the day, and the night, at the local pub.

'We reckon we need to move out soon and rent somewhere. This place is getting a bit too cramped for us,' offered an enthusiastic Devon.

'You think?' came the catty response from Amie, a response she regretted as soon as she uttered it.

Arlo gave her a death stare and dropped her hand, standing up so suddenly that Amie flinched. 'All right, enough stuffing around, the truck is due in half an hour, and we got prep to do.'

Amie and Mel looked at each other concerned, swallowed hard and asked simultaneously, 'The truck?'

Soon enough, the four were hiding behind a large dumpster in a back alley. The twins had found some clothes from a charity bin and made everyone dress in them. Amie was particularly upset, as she was wearing old clothes that could have belonged to anyone, and she was dressed completely out of fashion. But the boys had listened to the girls; they'd carefully planned every step of this attack. If there were any security cameras, the balaclavas and the strange wardrobe would confuse the police and keep the attention off the boys and their slightly unwilling accomplices.

The girls were scared. They didn't have a chance to talk

to each other, the boys never left them alone. But their eyes told each other just how scared they really were. They were relatively fine with the ATM robberies. They seemed like victimless crimes. But now their boyfriends were talking about sending a lightning bolt into an armoured truck full of security guards. No matter how scared they were, or how wrong they thought it was, neither were prepared to say no to the boys they'd grown to both love and fear.

The boys had always thought it'd be great to pull off an armed burglary. For months they'd planned how they would do it. They thought the teachers at school couldn't call them stupid anymore if they saw how detailed their plans were. They'd been watching the same trucks for a long time, recording the times the trucks arrived with vans full of cash. This had always been such a fantasy for them; they would sit out in the backyard till all hours talking about how rich they'd be after they pulled such a job. They always thought it would remain a fantasy, another unfulfilled dream in a lifetime of letdowns. Now with their power, they could actually become as wealthy as they always wanted.

The boys knew the girls were scared, and they probably didn't want to join in. Devon wanted to make a life with Mel; he was surprised at how much he cared for her. But if she wanted to be with him, she had to know this was who he was. He was a twin, and his brother always came first. Arlo liked Amie and hoped she would stick around, but he knew if he were honest, she was only there because of the powerful man she helped him become.

The boys' journal said that the truck would arrive between 2pm and 2.30, and right at 2.17, it turned the corner and headed straight for the local T.A.B — and straight for them.

'Game faces on, time to show them what we can do!'

The balaclavas were pulled down, Mel struggling with

hers. Her sweat made the acrylic material tough to pull down. Amie could see how petrified Mel was, and for the first time ever, she sent all her best wishes to her unlikely partner in crime. She held Mel's hand tightly and noticed tears beginning to soak into Mel's balaclava.

Arlo was so focused on the truck and couldn't see the panic of the girls, but Devon was more than aware. He simply placed his hand onto her shoulder in a supportive touch, which began glowing a dark blue, 'Everything will be good,' he added.

The light, the support, and Devon's words stopped Mel's tears but not her fears.

The truck pulled up in front of the T.A.B, the drivers casually chatting, thinking today was just like any other. They were taught to be vigilant, and they were, to an extent. But nothing could prepare them for what was about to happen.

As soon as Arlo saw the brake lights and heard the screech of the armoured truck's tyres, he yelled for them to start.

The four stepped from behind the dumpster, wearing mismatched dark clothes and balaclavas. They formed hands with military precision, and immediately the raw adrenaline coursing through their veins mixed with the dark-blue electricity that rose from deep inside them. The lightning shot out from the darkened alley, and within a moment, it crashed into the back of the truck. Sparks flew, a fire started, and the truck was thrown into the air, landing partially over the gutter. Screams were heard through the street, and people panicked, running away as fast as they could.

Suddenly, the foursome sprinted straight for the totalled truck.

Arlo and Devon were in front, with the girls trying to keep up. Mel ran through her tears. Amie, however, was terrified but strangely invigorated.

'Hurry up,' screamed Arlo; he needed the girls if things went awry.

Soon enough he was at the back of the truck, which burst open with thick, dark smoke billowing from inside. He tore open the door with ease. A security guard lay inside. He was barely conscious, but still fumbled for his gun.

'Don't think about it, mate, or this time you'll be the one blown up,' yelled Arlo.

The guard knew he meant it.

Devon was soon standing next to him, and the pair were shovelling money into the large backpacks they had brought. Arlo practically tossed Amie inside the truck where she also scavenged through the large bags and piles of cash. Her future flashed before her eyes, and she smiled — she was going to be filthy rich.

Mel was less enthusiastic in taking part. She stood watching the twins and Amie forage through the wreckage of the armoured truck. She felt disgusted by them, but also in herself. She knew, however, when they'd hand over her share of the loot, she'd happily take and spend it.

It was fortunate Mel was standing back from the action, as she saw one of the security guards falling out of the driver's seat. He had a large bloody gash on his forehead and a steely determination in his face. He was gripping his gun for dear life and was pointing it towards the back of the truck.

Devon finished loading one bag and was putting it down so he could begin filling another when his head poked around the corner and the guard aimed his gun, firing.

Mel jumped forward, screaming for her boyfriend. Defensively she placed her palm up as she reached for Devon. It seemed so futile — there was no way he could escape being shot. With one hand up, in a last-ditch effort, Mel grabbed Devon with her other hand. A dark-blue wall of electricity shot up around the pair, protecting them from harm. The bullet hit the field of electricity and immediately began to disintegrate before harmlessly falling to the asphalt.

Devon turned to Mel. She had saved his life, and he was so thankful. Even through the madness, he leaned across and kissed her, increasing the intensity of the beautiful force field that lazily hung in the air.

Arlo stood in shock when he heard the gunshot; he was positive his brother was a goner. Even he was surprised by the increasing power of the magic Devon and Mel were creating. As soon as he saw Devon was okay, he grabbed hold of Amie, pulling her from the truck with great force. Arlo scooped her up, grabbing her hands with such ferocity it sent pain through her whole body. She may be in pain but didn't dare breath a word. With his other hand, Arlo grabbed his brother's and again the dark-blue lightning bolt shot from the joined hands. The bolt jetted towards the force field, which seemed to open around the bolt as it charged through.

The guard could see the bolt coming for him, but there was no time to move. The lightning hit him in the chest, bursting into flames of red and blue on impact, and he fell to the ground.

Mel began crying; she knew she had just helped kill a man. Devon also stood in shock, while Amie was busy tending to her wounds.

Arlo, however, still had his game face on. 'Grab the bags and let's go before someone else starts shooting at us.'

With this, the four ran just as the third guard crawled from the passenger side of the truck. A security guard also ran from inside the building, stopping suddenly at the sight before him.

It was too late.

The four were inside the car that Arlo and Devon had

stolen earlier that day. Balaclavas were ripped off and small injuries were examined as Arlo tore through the back streets to safety.

Devon looked at the money, his sobbing girlfriend in the backseat, then back at the mayhem and smoke he could see in the distance. 'What the hell just happened?'

Arlo smirked and proudly stated, 'We're Gods now!'

CHAPTER NINETEEN: MADISON & KYLE

'I think you've got some major explaining to do,' stated Madison. She was the self-proclaimed leader of her secret group, and she didn't like losing control. Who was this new kid, and why was he suddenly able to create electricity with Parker — that was *her* job? Madison could feel the jealousy growing, and she didn't like it.

'I don't know how it happened, it just did,' explained Kyle. He had his own questions, but most prevalent on his mind was: why did they call in some girl who seemed to hate them? The type of girl that made Kyle's life hell back in Adelaide.

'No, pretty boy, I'm talking about the fact that this is your first day and you've already managed to infiltrate our secret group,' barked Madison. Too many people were starting to learn the truth.

'And you've been making a beeline for Parker, I've been watching you all day,' added Griffin, relieved Madison seemed to share his doubts.

Parker was ready to leap forward and defend this cute boy, but she saw his eyes, those eyes that seemed to speak directly to Parker. Was she wrong? Had she fallen under his spell and not recognised a deception because of her infatuation?

'I promise you, it's nothing sinister,' Kyle promptly responded, 'it's really not.' Kyle then went ahead and told his story, his full, unabridged story, ugly scars and all.

Parker noticed his eyes change again, and she saw the pain and knew he was telling the truth.

'I never knew it would be so wonderful, that light; it's so beautiful,' said Kyle with amazement.

Madison was surprised she believed him, strange as his story sounded. Then again, nothing seemed normal anymore. Griffin believed him too, but trust was still a long way off. Parker totally believed him, but she was crestfallen that he hadn't liked her after all, he was just using her for her powers.

'So that's why you wanted to hang around me? I should have guessed.'

'No, that's not it at all. I really do —'

There was a knock at the door.

Julia Bennett was trying to open it. The door slightly opened before hitting the chair that was blocking the entrance. 'Parker Bennett, why is this door blocked? We have no locks on our doors for a reason!' For the first time today, Julia was regretting her decision to leave four teenagers alone in a bedroom. With no immediate answer from inside the room, Julia pushed harder against the door, ready to use her shoulder for added strength. Just as she applied pressure, the door opened from the inside, and Julia came crashing into the room, almost losing her footing and falling to the floor. She was not happy.

'Alistair was doing his usual trick and kept annoying us, so I had to lock him out.'

'We'll talk about this later.' Julia was partially annoyed and partially embarrassed by her spill. But she was still able to realise now was probably not the time to interrogate her usually sensible daughter. 'Your English teacher is on the phone.'

'Ms Power?' asked Parker, while sharing her bewildered expression with Madison.

'Yes, maybe I should ask her about this mystery assignment?'

Parker walked to the lounge room. *Why is Ms Power calling me?* What started as a secret pact between Madison and herself was now a five-way secret; she was sure something would have to give.

Madison and the boys followed her closely. Parker was glad Madison was between her and Kyle. She was now confused as to how she felt about him.

As soon as she picked up the receiver and greeted her teacher, Tina spoke quickly, not wanting to waste any more time. 'Turn on the TV now.'

With great resistance from Alistair, Parker grabbed the TV remote, changing the channel from a cartoon to the news bulletin. A reporter stood in front of police tape, and behind it lay a totalled armoured truck, still being hosed down by the fire brigade. Smoke billowed into the polluted sky and police officers were busily attending to the crime scene.

The attractive reporter was interviewing a witness. Dressed in a power suit matched with perfect hair and immaculate make up, she earnestly held up her microphone to the older gentleman. It was immediately obvious he hadn't spent the same amount of time on his personal grooming.

'I'd just put some money down on number five in the eighth and was heading down to my local when the truck pulls up. Next thing there's this massive bolt of blue fire coming out of nowhere; it blew the truck up.'

Parker turned to Madison, uncertain as to what was happening.

Kyle was stunned; there were others like them?

'Then these four people in masks came running up and took all the money. One of the guards started shooting, and they killed him. They must've had some kind of crazy arse weapon, cause they set him alight!' the witness exclaimed.

Parker and Madison instinctively held hands; fear drawing them together again. It seemed now they felt safest when they knew they were near each other. They were still watching the screen so intently they didn't realise their hands were glowing a royal blue colour. Griffin's heart skipped a beat as he saw the intensity of their light building. He quickly stood in front of them, trying to block the view of Parker's mother and brother. He tried to get their attention without drawing any attention to them. He didn't want to risk touching them, his touch would no doubt make the illumination stronger.

Madison caught him staring in her peripheral vision, turning to him with a disgusted glare till she realised why he was invading her personal space. She quickly snatched her hand free, the light dissipating immediately. Parker looked down confused, only catching the tail end of the blue glow and realising they needed to be more careful.

Parker tried to convince her mother they could walk the fifteen minutes to Tina's house, but Julia was not going to let her daughter out of her sight just yet. The car ride over was filled with uncomfortable silences, and all of them gladly bundled out of the car on arrival at Tina's place.

'This seems highly unlikely that a teacher would ask four students over to her house,' Julia said when Tina opened the door.

'I'm helping them with some important work,' Tina answered back without hesitation.

'This mysterious assignment that has them locking

themselves in Parker's room?' Julia knew something was wrong here; she just couldn't put her finger on it.

Tina tried to convince her that it was about the assignment, and begrudgingly she left, but only after Tina promised to personally drop Parker back home.

Parker felt the relief as her mother drove off, but she also knew her mother was only a minor problem in the big scheme of things.

Tina was at first unsure why Kyle had joined them, but after a full story and a demonstration, the five sat down for a planning session.

'Mr Baxter's car, the ATM robberies, now this truck robbery and murder, they have to be connected. You aren't the only ones with powers, and we need to find these others, and we need to find them fast.' Tina laid down the facts as she poured her students some tea.

'These freaks are gonna get us caught.' Self-preservation was never far from Madison's thoughts. 'We need to track them down, and we need to stop them.'

This idea terrified Parker, she was no superhero. She'd already stopped two felons this month, and that was two felons too many.

'There's four of you now. You need to pool your powers, get stronger, get sharper and be ready for anything.'

Parker thought Ms Power may have seen too many movies, but she did have a point. This battle had seen its first fatality, and Parker was worried it would not be the last.

That afternoon, the four practised, all under the watchful eye of Tina. They were surprised at how intense the electricity became when all four joined hands. Tina knew it was lucky her son was spending the night at a friend's place, because for a short while she was worried her roof might be ripped off and her house burnt down at the hands of a beautiful blue flame.

Night was setting in, and the four were both mentally and psychically drained. They were preparing to go home, Parker still avoiding direct conversation with Kyle. She was happy he'd joined their team, but she was still unsure how she felt about him.

Tina was preparing to drive them home when she made her final point for the evening. 'The thing is kids; these other people could be anyone. Other students, teachers, parents. They could be close friends, and we have no idea. We need to be vigilant and watch everyone, because if they discover your secret before we discover theirs, this could end very badly.'

The four stopped. They knew Tina was right; everyone was a suspect. School tomorrow was going to be a whole new affair.

CHAPTER TWENTY: AMY & BEAU

School now seemed a foreign place to Parker. As she entered the grounds in the morning, she examined the faces of all her fellow students. Any one of them could share the same power as her and was using it with deadly force. Everything had been so intense lately that Parker could barely remember the simple life she led before.

Beau could sense something was wrong — some days his best friend had a dark cloud hanging above her. Today, this cloud seemed to be extra dark. 'So, I'm guessing that things with Kyle didn't go well last night?'

Then there was Kyle; she hadn't really had the chance to think about all that was happening with him. She still wanted to believe that he really did like her for her, but she was worried part of her would always doubt his motives. Was he just using her for her powers?

'Parker? You with me?' Parker didn't answer, and Beau was getting worried.

Before she could answer, Kyle arrived. He was full of smiles, and Beau was full of confusion.

Kyle had spent his first evening learning how to conduct electricity from his hands, and he honestly believed that it could have been the best night of his life. 'I had a great time last night, Parker, that was really special.'

Parker smiled and then looked sheepishly across to Beau; she hoped he didn't get the wrong impression.

But it was too late; Beau had already added one and one and gotten five. 'Oh my God, you two didn't —'

Before he could even finish that sentence, both Parker and Kyle jumped in with a loud and emphatic 'No!' Both were embarrassed and going red, and Beau was more than a little bewildered. He wasn't quite sure what question to ask next. He didn't receive a call from Parker last night as promised, just a text stating tiredness and promising a full brief in the morning. Morning was now here, and no brief was apparent.

While today was supposed to be about Parker being suspicious of all around her, it was Beau who could sense that something was not quite right.

Before he could begin his interrogation, Mel arrived. Mel looked tired and emotional. Her eyes were red and had big black bags. As soon as she saw her friends, she burst into tears and threw herself into a hug with Parker. Beau and Parker shared a concerned glance, but they were also confused. Mel was not usually the emotional one in the group; in fact, they'd never seen her cry before.

'Mel, what's wrong?' asked Parker. She hated seeing her friend in so much pain.

Mel pulled away from Parker's embrace; she was starting to leave tear stains on her friend's school shirt, her real friend. Parker was not using her for powers like she was worried her boyfriend was. Mel didn't think she'd cried so much in her life, not even when her grandfather or her dog had died. 'Everything's terrible, completely terrible.'

Mel wanted to bring Parker and Beau's presents. She had deserted them lately. Yes, she may be number three in a group of three, but Parker and Beau made no secret of that. And they loved her, she knew that. Mel had spent most of her night staring at her share of the money, the blood money she helped steal. She couldn't bring herself to spend it. Luckily, she hadn't, because if Parker received some expensive gift, suspicions would certainly have been raised.

Parker felt empathy for the friend she'd neglected. She was beginning to feel very guilty.

Both Parker and Beau pleaded with Mel to tell them what was wrong.

Mel wanted to blurt out everything — the twins, the power, the robbery — but she knew she couldn't. She didn't think for a second that they could possibly understand what she was going through. She searched her mind for an excuse, any excuse. Plus, she knew if she breathed a word about the twins and they found out, her own life could be in danger. 'I lost my mum's bracelet and my parents have been fighting. I think they may get a divorce.'

The friends comforted her till she settled down, and Mel started feeling okay again. Kyle looked on shocked — women were a foreign concept to him, and today proved it.

Mel enjoyed being back in the sanctuary of her social group. When she started laughing at Beau's bad jokes, they knew she would be all right.

The four started heading for the lockers. Mel was feeling better, and Kyle talked with Beau while looking longingly at Parker. Parker, meanwhile, continued to look in the eyes of everyone she passed. Anyone could be the person she was intent on finding. She was busy watching Henry Cruz walk with Grayson. She'd never liked him; he was very fond of teasing Beau on a regular basis. He'd also been absent the day before and always seemed to have the latest tech gadgets. Today he was flashing around a brand-new smartwatch. As much as Madison might not like it, Henry was on the top of her suspect list. Plus, she kind of liked the idea of seeing him in jail. Parker was so busy imagining Henry being dragged out of class in handcuffs that she hadn't seen Griffin leaning against her locker.

'When did you become the school sex symbol?' Beau laughed.

Parker was confused until she saw Griffin smiling at her. She looked around for Madison; if she witnessed this, she would be ropable. With no Madison in sight, Parker allowed herself to smile back. Griffin's grin was comforting. Parker moved quickly ahead, just so she could chat to Griffin alone. She saw the disappointment on Kyle's face as she leaned in to whisper to Griffin, 'You realise if Madison sees us together, she'll find a way to have us electrocute ourselves?' Parker smiled as she joked, but thought if Madison heard this idea, she would probably will it to happen.

'We're friends, right?' asked Griffin, without the hint of the smile Parker was wearing as a mask.

'Of course we are.' Parker was shocked that Griffin thought they weren't friends. She was closer to him than most other people at the school; they shared an amazing bond, and secret.

'Well, if we're friends, why can't I hang around you at school?'

It was a valid question, and Parker could only answer with the rehearsed speech about Madison's theories. 'But you let the new kid join your group?'

Griffin was tired of being a loner. He had reasons for pulling away from his friends years before, but now he wanted to be part of a group again, not just behind closed doors. He wanted to be a part of Parker's group.

Before she could answer, she saw Madison enter from

the other end of the hallway, and a slight panic took over her. Yes, she may have liked Madison, liked the friendship that was building, but she was also terrified of her and her social standing.

Madison wasn't looking at them though; like Parker, she was searching the eyes of everyone she passed. She walked down the middle of the hallway, flanked on either side by her generals: Amy and Amie. People stopped conversations and moved so she could pass. Madison was the school enigma, and everyone was desperate to learn her mysteries.

She had never even glanced at most of the boys from the school, so now that she was looking intently into their eyes, looking for a criminal mastermind, hearts began to flutter. More boys were ready to declare their undying love, and Madison couldn't find one suspect. This upset her. She was the one with the powers, the one in charge of her secret group, and she wanted it to stay that way.

Madison barely noticed Amy move past her. She'd just been staring into the eyes of a Year 8 boy who was now convinced he was about to marry the school beauty. He even had to place his folder in front of his pants to avoid embarrassment.

Amy began to walk straight towards Parker's group, and Parker — for a small second — wondered whether Madison sent her to drag her away from Griffin. Instead, Amy, full of smiles, walked straight up to Beau and hugged him, tightly.

Madison stopped in her tracks, confused.

Amie and Mel stole a quick glance, a knowing look before turning away. They hadn't yet talked about what had happened, and both were desperate to chat, even though part of them hoped they'd never see the other again. Now was not the time for their debrief.

Madison and Parker also glanced at each other, not sure

what was happening. It was then that Madison saw Griffin standing with Parker, and she scowled.

Parker looked away, busted.

'Oh my God, that Spotify playlist you made me was amazing. I played it all night. I made a playlist for you too,' gushed Amy.

In return, Beau gave her an appreciative smile; the rest stared in shock and amazement.

'Um, Amy, what are you doing?' asked a bewildered Amie. There was an order in the school, and while she might have to talk to Mel out of school time, Mel was dead to her in the hallways.

'Beau and I have lived next door to each other our whole lives, and we used to play as kids, and then we grew apart. But lately, you girls are always busy, and I hate being by myself. Yesterday, neither of you answered your phones. Then I went to your house, Madison, and your mum said you were at Amie's. But when I went to Amie's house, your mum said you were at Madison's.'

Madison and Amie peered across to each other, caught out.

Suspicions were now aroused.

'And my mum was going for coffee at Beau's house, so I went along. Do you know how funny Beau is? And he knows everything about music, and I mean *everything*. Ask him anything.'

There seemed to be a change in the air, and they could all feel it.

Parker smiled nervously at Beau, who smiled back with joy in his eyes. One night of gossip with Amy could never replace a lifetime of friendship, no matter how popular Amy was at school.

Madison felt slightly embarrassed. She'd never felt Amy

was overly intelligent, but today she probably respected her more than ever before. Madison liked Parker, she liked her a lot, but she never felt she could be friends with her in the school halls. She caught Parker's eye and the pair both wondered if anything would ever be the same again. The power of the electricity seemed to be changing the school ... and everyone in it.

CHAPTER TWENTY-ONE: MRS LING

Gina Ling hated school discos. She hated the music, she hated the teenage hormones, and most importantly, she hated the shocking overdose of men's cologne. Mr Baxter organised the roster for the evening and was fielding all kinds of excuses from teachers as to why they couldn't work. The Sports teacher Mr Travers was dealing with the death of his grandmother, an excuse he'd used for the previous dance. The Drama teacher Ms Harrison used all her acting training and cried on cue. She was a mother who needed to be home with her sick son, even if he was twenty-one. The child card was played by many teachers, so the childless Mrs Ling was volunteered, much to her disdain.

Even worse for Mrs Ling was who she was rostered on with. She wasn't a particular fan of Tina Power. She thought she was overly emotional and didn't like her teaching style. And since the History staff room had been infested with fleas, the History teachers had been squashed in with the English teachers. Tina Power was also acting extra weird lately. They had a strange conversation where Tina was asking about Gina's movements for the previous afternoon. Gina was not looking forward to spending an evening with her.

The students piled into the school hall, the music already blaring. The dance floor was full of students, and Mrs Ling was already pulling apart students who were too close. Those kissing were threatened with all manner of detentions. Mrs Ling stood next to Tina and the Maths teacher, Mr Anderson, along the wall; she was surprised that Tina was not talking their ear off, like she usually would.

Instead, Tina was desperately searching the crowd with her eyes. Unlike the other teachers, she wasn't looking for inappropriate touches or smuggled in alcohol, she was looking for the hint of dark-blue electricity. She was sure something was going to happen tonight.

Parker entered the school hall with trepidation. Beau had talked her into going to the school dance once before and she'd hated it completely. She loved dancing with Beau; he could always move so well to the music. Then Grayson and Henry came across to them and made particularly nasty gay jokes to Beau and he'd wanted to leave immediately.

A year later and she was back. Beau stood nervously next to her, Mel on his other side. She squeezed his shoulder for support. Beau hated that he feared the school dance — music was his passion, and the Neanderthals from his school took away some of that love. He'd promised never to walk through the door of a dance again, and Parker solemnly agreed. So, it came as a huge shock when she had pushed for him to attend.

Kyle and Griffin stood on the other side of Parker. They were attempting a friendship, mainly for Parker. But neither completely trusted the other, and their arrangement was certainly an uneasy one. Both had never been to a school dance before and were more nervous than they let on.

Together the five stood, not quite ready to walk onto the

dance floor, or even attempt to claim a section of the wall. Tina encouraged them all to attend, certain their opponents would be in attendance too. Madison had quickly agreed, she loved the school dance, so no argument from the other three in the group was going to deter her.

Suddenly, Amy emerged from the sea of dancing teens. She was wearing such a revealingly low-cut dress that Mrs Ling had considered sending her home to change. Her face was again full of smiles for Beau as she hugged him one more time. 'I am so glad you came, we have to dance, now!'

Beau barely had time to protest before he was on the middle of the dance floor with Amy dancing closely to him. Parker smiled, she thought Amy was going to end up very disappointed. She was also glad Beau finally seemed happy and at ease as his body moved perfectly to the music.

Then Parker saw Madison. She was being draped by her dopey boyfriend Grayson. His hands were wandering all over Madison. However, her mind was somewhere else. Parker was quite taken aback by how Madison looked. Parker went to little effort; Beau had to convince her to wear mascara. Whereas Madison looked ready for another of her many glamorous Instagram posts. Parker could see Grayson's desperate attempts to claim his territory. She looked amazing, and every schoolboy in the room had noticed.

Next to them were Amie and Henry. Henry's hands were exploring Amie's tender frame, he was very much enjoying himself. Amie thought that if Arlo could see him doing this, Henry would be shot with a lightning bolt. Henry's hand made its way up Amie's thigh, Amie barely registering. Mrs Ling quickly arrived with a sermon about proper social behaviour and etiquette, even quoting a statistic about teenage pregnancies. She was pleased with her efforts and satisfied that all parties had separated.

Tina was starting to get impatient. The whole student body was basically in the same area, and she knew the culprits were somewhere in the hall. She managed to have a quick word with Parker — Parker relaying her suspicions about Henry.

Then when they turned to see him, he was gone.

Amy was back from dancing with Beau, all excited and full of details Madison and Amie weren't interested in.

Parker scanned the room, spotting Grayson. He was in the process of bullying some poor unfortunate Year 7 kids. Other moronic friends of his were acting as his back up, laughing at every unintelligent taunt falling from his mouth. But not Henry.

Henry was smarter than most gave him credit for. He'd watched the Thomas twins make a plethora of cash at every school disco and thought it would be just as easy for him to take their place now they were suspended. Henry's brother Jack was a university student with a part-time job at a bottle store and was acting as his supplier, a supplier demanding a rather large cut.

Henry had studied the model for success the Thomas twins had used for years, even setting up his operation in the same pocket behind the school hall. Arlo always used Devon as his teacher scout; Henry had his protégé doing the job, the ever-loyal Clark Teo. Clark was the youngest in the year and was always desperate to fit in. Henry liked to exploit that.

Henry's first night as the school's beer baron was a smashing success. He'd gone through half his stock and had already received a large order for a sixteenth birthday party the following week. And everyone was so complimentary and appreciative of his 'service with a smile'. They didn't have to be scared of Henry like they were with the Thomas twins. Sometimes you'd get your alcohol from them with no dramas, but sometimes it'd be served with a side order of ridicule and abuse, and occasionally you'd get a beating for your trouble. Henry saw himself as a professional and knew how to run a good business — he saw himself as a future millionaire.

Henry's downfall was no doubt his cockiness and his naïve belief that he'd outsmarted everyone. It was not a teacher who brought Henry crashing back to earth, but the Thomas twins, who Henry had completely underestimated. Henry thought their suspension would bring an end to their backyard moonshine operation, when in fact it'd made them more determined to hit back at Baldy Baxter. Totalling his prized car was never going to be enough, not now, not since Arlo had declared himself a deity.

The twins emerged from the darkness of the evening carrying a large box of spirits. They arrived so suddenly that Clark at first thought he was hallucinating from the rather large swig of bourbon he'd just consumed. But when the twins were right on him, he felt the very strong urge to pee his pants. Arlo grimaced at Clark, and he was off. He was much more frightened of Arlo than he was of Henry, so he ran. He sprinted back inside to the safety of the disco lights and mirror balls, leaving Henry alone and defenceless.

'Pleasure doing business with you, Costa, and remember, anytime, anyplace, I can hook you up with beverages.' Henry was finishing a business deal; he shook Costa's hand, looked firmly in his eyes and smiled. In this moment he truly believed he was a top businessman.

'Oi, idiot, what do you think you're doing?' asked Arlo, adding a few more colourful words for affect. Arlo was angry, he snarled, and Costa took off, dropping his newly acquired vodka. It smashed on the concrete, but he didn't stop to mourn his lose; he just hurried in the same direction that Clark had travelled.

'You're supposed to be suspended.' Henry was hoping there was no fear in his voice.

'As if that was gonna stop us,' added Devon, before letting his brother take the lead.

'And you're in OUR spot with OUR customers, so we're gonna have to shut you down.' Arlo kicked over the box of leftover alcohol Henry had been happily dipping into all evening. The bottles smashed, and the liquid made a path for the grass.

'I'll go tell Baldy you're here. You'll be expelled.' Henry tried to sound tough despite his sheer terror. He'd heard that Arlo killed his childhood dog because the dog kept barking through the night. Arlo had made that story up to gain notoriety, and it had worked, because Henry believed every word.

'How do you reckon he'll like hearing about your little business venture here, hey?' Devon laughed.

Arlo joined in; they weren't as stupid as people thought.

'Baldy rates me; I kicked the winning goal in the soccer championship. Who's he gonna believe? Then you'll be expelled, and I'll have your business.' Henry sniggered this time, his bravado was building. He was feeling victorious.

'I've killed people, you know? And you're next on my list.' There was no smile from Arlo this time, or from Devon. He meant every single word, and Henry knew it.

As sweat was permeating from every pore of his athletic body, Henry didn't hesitate. He used his skills as the school's sprint star and bolted for the same entrance the other boys had used.

Arlo and Devon took pursuit, but Henry caught them off guard, and he was way too fast. Arlo kicked the wall, hurting his foot a little. He wanted vengeance, and he wanted it now.

Mel was laughing with Kyle and Griffin when her phone beeped. At first, she was unsure about the new additions to their group, but she liked talking to the boys. And plus, with more joining their group, the more popular they looked. Her smile disappeared though when she felt her phone vibrate in her pocket; she didn't need to read the message. She knew what it was going to say: *Babe, I'm outside in the usual spot, I need you now.*

Yesterday had been, by far, the biggest day in Mel's reasonably short life. She'd gone from robbery to murder, two things she couldn't have even comprehended before meeting the twins. With a sleepless night under her belt and the clarity of sunlight, Mel decided she needed to get on the wagon and give up Devon and forget her powers. She promised herself. But that afternoon when she arrived home from school and was rifling through her wardrobe for an outfit to the dance, there was a knock at her window.

Before she could tell him to go away, Devon removed the fly screen and was casually climbing through. She threatened to scream, she threatened to call the police, but Devon just stood before her. Fear then gripped Mel — what if Arlo was just behind? She never wanted to see him again.

Mel wished her parents were home; she could have called out to them. If Devon heard her family hurtling into the room, he'd have to leave. Instead, he stood watching her, with a slight smile on his face. Mel hated that he was grinning, she always thought he looked so handsome when he smiled. She knew the boys were twins, but Devon was better looking, especially when he smiled.

'I'm sorry about yesterday, we never meant for it to go that way.' Devon was calm as he spoke.

'But it did! Someone is dead, and we were the ones who killed him. I don't think I want to do this anymore.' Tears began to well in Mel's eyes, but she was determined — this had to end.

'But, Mel, I love you.'

And with those three short words, Mel forgave him. Her heart melted, and she forgot the look on the face of the security guard as they aimed their lightning bolt at him. For the first time ever, without the touch of her boyfriend, Mel began to slightly radiate. Her skin began to glow a soft blue, Devon smiled, and Mel looked down amazed at her own skin.

Devon had quickly stepped forward and the pair began to kiss, more intently and passionately than ever before. The pair made love that afternoon for the first time, the dark-blue electricity never far from the tiny bedroom. A neighbour saw the blue glow through the window and wondered what Mel was watching on TV.

Devon left that evening, just as Mel's parent's car pulled up in the driveway. He climbed from the window backwards, not taking his eyes off Mel. He kissed her softly one last time, the dark-blue light still happily floating between them. 'You and me, Mel, always.'

Mel now excused herself from her friends, pretending to head to the toilets, and she crept outside. She still didn't want to see Arlo, but she was dying to see Devon. She wondered how she could feel so very differently about two people who looked so alike.

When she arrived in the usual spot, Amie was already standing with the boys. She could smell the strong aroma of alcohol mixed with the smell of fear.

'We just love waiting around for you,' stated Amie, sarcastically.

Arlo was ropable, ranting and raving, and Mel was petrified. Devon could see her turmoil and gripped her hand tightly. Arlo's ego had reached ridiculous levels, he was believing his own press and was genuinely offended that someone would dare try and fleece his business. But it wasn't just Henry he was angry with; he also wanted revenge against all his former customers who turned their backs on him. His rant soon moved onto the teachers that had done him wrong, especially Baldy Baxter. He said there was only one thing they could do ...

A tear slowly escaped from the side of Mel's eye.

'We need to burn down the school hall.'

Amie immediately screamed with glee; this was a fantasy she hadn't yet thought of.

Devon had to stop Mel, who subconsciously started backing away. He could see her panic, and it surprised him how much it affected him; but his brother had made a decision, and that was what was going to happen.

'But all those people in there, some of them are my friends.' Mel began to cry.

Arlo felt his temper rise. He wanted to yell at her, and he wanted to slap her, but he knew he needed her. 'There's like a 150 fire exits in the hall. It'll scare the hell of them, that's all.'

The thing Mel didn't know was that before the twins had messaged their respective girlfriends, they'd blocked most of the fire exits. But they knew many would still be able to escape through the large doors in the front of the hall. This wasn't about killing all their school mates; this was about causing the maximum panic. If a few lives were lost, their point would be driven home even harder: don't mess with the Thomas twins.

Mel still needed to be convinced. Arlo was getting more and more frustrated, and at one point Mel thought she was only seconds from a back hander. Amie began to goad her as well, calling her names and ridiculing her so she'd 'spark' up. It was Devon who finally convinced her to take part. He stepped a few paces away from the others, took her hands, kissed her forehead, looked deeply into her hazel eyes, and whispered, 'As long as you're with me, I'll make sure nothing bad ever happens to you.'

Henry returned to the school disco drenched in a lather of sweat and with fear etched all over his face. Parker was sure he was the one they were looking for. Amy came back to ask Beau to step back onto the dance floor, but he declined her kind offer, not wanting to leave Parker. But Parker wanted to follow Henry, so she convinced him to hit that dance floor once more.

With Amy clutching his hand, Beau was begrudgingly dragged back into the sea of bad dancers. He saw Xavier dancing with Hannah McGinty, the school's resident 'model'. She only just returned to complete her HSC after walking at Fashion Week. Everyone thought they were a perfect couple and would produce the world's best-looking children, even though the pair claimed they were 'just friends'. Xavier caught Beau's stare and smiled back.

'We need to go follow Henry, he's up to something,' stated Parker to Kyle and Griffin. She was hoping she could catch him in the act, and with the boys, she had some protection. She looked across to Tina, who stood with the other teachers. Tina nodded her approval; she had noticed Henry enter flustered and knew exactly what Parker was going to do.

The three pushed their way through the crowd, on the way passing Madison, who was in a lip lock with Grayson.

Beau saw the three heading into the sea of people and wondered why Parker would take Griffin with her to have a talk with Kyle.

Parker followed Henry into the backstage area of the school hall, then saw him duck into the male dressing rooms. This was an out of bounds area during the dance, and Mr

Baxter had laid down the law that trouble would rain down on anyone found backstage.

Henry must be up to something.

The Parker of old, the Parker of a few short weeks ago, wouldn't dare barge in on a school bully. And she certainly wouldn't be as excited as she was in this moment. With the boys acting as her heavies, Parker charged through the dressing room door. She wasn't sure if she would find Henry using the dark equivalent of her ability, or if Henry was waiting ready to attack. She would never have suspected what they really did find.

Henry, on the floor, head in his hands, crying his eyes out. 'What the hell do you want?' Henry yelled through his tears.

'I know what you did, and I'm not going to let you get away with it!' Parker was channelling Madison, and even the boys were impressed with her tenacity. Parker was positive she'd found her villain.

Henry just thought he was the worst businessman in the world. First, the school bullies left him crying like a baby, and now even the school dweeb was taking pot shots. 'You're a bit late, dork; they've already thrown me out.' Henry wiped his tears away; this could be the single most embarrassing moment of his life.

Parker's mind start racing, as did the boys. What did Henry mean? How many were in this group? And just who were they? Before she could ask these questions, they heard screaming from inside the hall, screams so loud it was drowning out the frantic dance music that was blaring through the hall.

Parker turned to both the boys — whatever was happening, it couldn't be good. Suddenly the music stopped, and the sound of teenagers screaming was the only sound echoing through the hall. A moment later the fire alarm sounded, and Parker and the boys, followed closely by Henry, ran from the dressing room. They could smell both the smoke and the panic filling the hall.

The four began to run down the steps, desperate to see what was happening in the hall. But after only a few steps, Parker could see the mayhem — the door to the hall burst open and panicked people started pouring through, led by an authoritative Mrs Ling.

'Quick, kids, through to the fire doors. There's no need to panic at all.' Mrs Ling stood with the door open as kids piled backstage, heading for the fire door.

Some screamed, some cried, some looked ready to urinate their pants, but all sprinted, desperate to escape the mayhem. Everything was so rushed that they barely noticed the four confused students they were passing, except Mrs Ling, who commanded them to not waste any more time and follow her to safety.

But they didn't, they needed to see for themselves what was happening. They ran into the hall and froze when they saw the sight before them. The side entrance to the hall was completely engulfed in flames and it was spreading faster than it should. The flames that leapt forward seemed tinged with a dark blue. Parker knew only one thing could have caused those blue flames.

The screams were now becoming deafening. Students and teachers were rushing for all available exits. The panic really began to set in, however, when students attempted to push open fire doors, but they couldn't budge them. Sheer terror was now gripping the hall as people worried that they wouldn't make it out alive. The roof was now covered in a river of dark-blue flames. People were falling over and being trampled as everyone raced for the one entrance available to them now. With the intensity of the flames getting stronger and stronger by the minute, there was no way everyone was going to make it out in time before the hall was engulfed entirely in flames.

Madison sprinted across to Parker, panic in her eyes. Grayson had just stepped over some younger kids to get out, but she let go of his hand, and he didn't even stop to grab it again. She knew she must find Parker and she must do something to help. Their amazing power could be used to save people. 'No one's looking, let's blast open one of these fire doors.'

'Are we sure we wouldn't just add to the fire's intensity?' Kyle voiced what the others were all thinking.

'We have to try or hardly anyone is going to survive.'

They'd never seen Madison show such sincerity or care for people, and they knew she was right.

The four ran to the nearest fire door; everyone else was panicking and attempting to exit out the front. There was no way they would be seen. They joined hands, never before holding hands so tightly. They gripped on for dear life, and quicker than ever before, the electricity shot from their hands. It burst from deep within them, breaking open the door, as if it knew what its purpose was. They had no time to admire their work; it would be hard to yell over the noise. In unison, they yelled out there was another door, and soon enough people headed to the door to escape the flames. Screaming teens running for their lives.

The four then ran across to another blocked exit and burst open another door, this time with even less effort. Ceiling beams were now falling, and the heat was intensifying; they couldn't make it to another door. But they were sure they'd done enough, as people were piling out of the three exits. Some were hurt, but at least they were outside. A number of students were hit by the flames and were lying on the grass in agony. In the distance, sirens could be heard. There was pandemonium everywhere.

Beau pushed through the crowd, Amy tailing him. He began to cry when he saw Parker unharmed, throwing his arms around her. 'Thank God you're all right. I was so worried when I couldn't find you.'

'I'm okay, a bit shaken, but I'm okay.' She'd never been so happy to hug her best friend.

Everyone stood back; the teachers pushing them as far away from the hall as they could. It was now falling down, engulfed entirely in flames. No one could turn away, as it was a mesmerising spectacle. More reunions were taking place — people finding friends and hugging them for dear life. Wounds were being attended to, and all were relieved they'd escaped.

Finally, Mel and Amie both arrived sheepishly. The girls couldn't believe what they had caused. The twins were now completely out of control. Mel cried again when she saw her friends.

Mr Anderson suddenly pushed through the students, panic overtaking him. 'Has anyone seen Mrs Ling?'

But no one had.

More names were being called out: Astra Greg, Julian Radcliffe, Raj Tandon, Donovan Wagner and Iris Yung.

Parker turned to Kyle and Griffin, the colour draining from her face. 'Those were the people who passed us backstage!'

CHAPTER TWENTY-TWO: TINA & JEREMY

School was cancelled on Friday. Instead of the playground being filled with students, it was filled with firemen and police officers. The school was a crime scene, and an investigation had begun.

One thing became apparent: Mrs Ling died a hero. Stories began surfacing from the students who survived the rush backstage. Few survived, but those who did stated solemnly that none would have survived without Mrs Ling. After they discovered the fire door was blocked, and no amount of charging was going to break it open, they tried to return to the hall. By that time, fire had engulfed the backstage area, and their path to freedom was obscured. Some students immediately crumbled emotionally, but not Mrs Ling. She grabbed the nearest fire extinguisher and tried her best to clear a path. Some students were able to sneak through before the roof collapsed straight on top of Mrs Ling.

The police were baffled, they could find no signs of accelerants, but other evidence was leading them to believe that this fire was certainly lit on purpose. They began calling it a homicide. The doors were barricaded from the outside, a chilling clue that the arsonist had sinister motives. The burn patterns also indicated they were similar to the fires which had occurred at the local ATMs and this week's armoured truck robbery. A task force was assembled, and the police were growing concerned that if this was the same perpetrator, their use of violence and disregard for human life was escalating.

While the students were given the Friday off school, the teachers were still required to attend. There was counselling available, and the police had many questions to ask. Tina received hugs and well wishes, but she just wanted to be left alone. She felt bad. She knew something was going to happen at the event, and while she could never have predicted something so large and so vile, she should have been able to stop it. She couldn't help but feel responsible for the lives that had been lost. She may not have been the biggest fan of Mrs Ling, but she respected her and knew she was going to miss her snarky glares and subtle jabs.

The police turned one of the science labs into a make-shift interview room. They were talking to teachers about who they thought could be responsible for such a deplorable act. They were also very keen to talk to the teachers in attendance at the dance. Mr Baxter and Mr Anderson shed little light; they hadn't seen anything. Tina was the next to be interviewed. She barely looked across at the police as she entered the science lab. She sat down, mind in another place, not really ready to answer any questions.

'Hello, Tina, do you remember me?'

Tina looked up at the officer and tried to scan her memory. The others were detectives in suits; he was the only uniformed officer in the room. He was quite handsome, in a straitlaced kind of way; she was sure she'd remember if they had met before.

'I don't blame you for not being sure. We met when you were a little out of it, after the robbery at the convenience store.'

Tina vaguely remembered the officer arriving just as she was being taken off to the hospital after the robbery. She also half remembered him visiting her in hospital, but it had been detectives who'd interviewed her about the robbery. So why was he here now asking the questions? 'You seem to be a long way from the Newtown precinct?'

'A task force needs a lot of officers. They were asking for volunteers, and plus, the arson boys are saying that the flame is like the one we found in that convenience store.'

Tina suddenly realised the dangers her kids were about to face.

Both Parker and Madison were surprised and slightly worried when their parents were phoned to bring them into the school on their day off. They became even more concerned when they spotted each other entering the school, parents in tow. At that moment, they'd forgotten they weren't supposed to be friends and headed straight for each other. So, while their parents politely said hello and pledged to abuse anyone who dared make the slightest negative comment about their children, the girls stole a moment.

'It doesn't look like they've asked anyone else here, do you reckon Power spilled?' asked Madison directly.

'No, she's solid, and the boys weren't called in. This is something else; I just don't know what though.'

Soon enough the pair were together in the science lab they hated so much. Science was not the forte for either, and they didn't like their science teacher, Ms Grech, who inhabited this room normally.

The police wanted to separate the pair, talk to them individually, but when the girls' mothers began to scream persecution, the girls were allowed a joint interview.

The detectives asked a few general questions about the

school disco fire, and the girls answered as truthfully as they could. They were in different areas when the fire started, both naming their alibis in case they were about to be accused of starting the fire. They also revealed they ended up in the same spot and were able to assist in pushing open the fire doors, no doubt helping to save their fellow students.

Then Jeremy came forward.

Both girls hadn't seen him sitting patiently in the corner, observing. They looked at each other puzzled as he came over to talk to them.

He sat down with a smile, breathed deeply, and began to talk slowly, not wanting to alarm the girls or scare them into silence. 'I'm hoping you remember me, girls?'

Madison didn't need to wait to see if Parker was going to answer, she knew she was the pair's self-appointed spokeswoman.

'Of course we do, you're the guy who thought we were banging that sweaty, ugly crim so we could rob a convenience store together.'

One of the detectives and both the girls' fathers chuckled a little, and Parker looked across in shock at the now smiling Madison, who was loving the spotlight.

'That's not what I thought at all. You were the victims there. But something always seemed a little strange to me.'

'Besides the fact that your boss was so terrified of my mother that he literally pushed us out the door?'

Madison's mum beamed with pride. Madison had a habit of sometimes being insolent, something she was often in trouble for. But how could she be angry with her daughter for being able to stand up to the police's bullying tactics?

'No, because of the forensics.' Jeremy was eager to wipe the smile off this teenager's face; she was really annoying him, and he knew she was hiding something. 'The crime lab had an interesting time with the scorch marks that were left in the convenience store after you miraculously stopped that very experienced criminal. Something happened in that store, and I want to find out what it was.'

Madison was ready to hit back, she was just searching her mind for the right insult when she was surprised to hear Parker jump in.

'Our teacher was with us when we were fired at, did you reinterview her? What did Ms Power have to say?'

Madison smiled widely. 'Yeah, what did Ms Power have to say?'

'She claims she didn't see anything but fear on your faces. She seems to think you girls are heroes. But here's the problem, ladies, our forensic team wasn't able to identify where those marks came from. The only thing they were really able to ascertain was that the fire was the same type that burnt the ATMs in your area, burnt the armoured truck this week and also torched your school hall last night. Why is that, ladies?' Jeremy was smiling inside; he could see the girls were, for the first time, speechless.

They were slowly starting to panic; they had no answer.

It was Julia Bennett who was ready to jump in this time. The neighbour's dog had started barking at 5am that morning, and she was angry, she was annoyed, and this officer was going to be the one who bared the brunt of her fury. 'So, let me get this straight, you think that these two young girls are some kind of pyromaniac criminal master-minds? Are you an idiot?'

Madison's mother didn't want to be outdone, she was ready to launch as well, not as a back-up singer to Julia Bennett, but as her duet partner. 'And wasn't that truck blown up during school hours? I think you'll find both of the girls were in school that day, ask anyone.'

'And those ATMs were blown up late at night; I can guarantee that our children were safely in their beds. Unlike other parents, we know exactly where our children are late at night. Shouldn't you be questioning the children who don't have good parents? Or are you just that desperate to pin these crimes on anyone, including innocent teenagers?'

The husbands smiled, they added the odd word of support, but they knew they were here to merely enjoy the show — and enjoy it they were.

The other detectives were now starting to get agitated; they had let this senior constable join their operation after claiming he had information that could help. All he'd given them so far was a massive headache.

'This will be the last time you'll try to harass our daughters, or I'll be calling the police commissioner,' threatened Madison's mum.

'And my boss' sister is one of the producers on *A Current Affair* — they love stories like this.' Julia was on a roll.

Madison's mum was over this intrusion into her family's life; she wanted out of there, and out of there now. The anger left her face and her eyes glazed over slightly, as emotion was taking control of her. 'You pulled my family away from our home at the worst possible time. Madison's brother has leukemia, and the doctors have given him weeks, maybe days. And because of this ridiculous interrogation, you are stealing time away with my son.'

Apologises were thick and fast from the lead detective, who jumped straight up. The last thing his department needed was negative press for taking a grieving family away from their dying son.

Jeremy was embarrassed, sure he would be fired from the task force.

The families were again quickly bundled out the door

with the promise of peace in the future and condolences to the O'Sullivan family.

As they walked to the car, everyone was silent, their victory hollow.

Parker then turned to Madison, whispering so their parents couldn't hear. 'I'm so sorry about Lachlan, I had no idea.'

'No one does, you're the first friend to know.' Madison wanted to smile at Parker, but she was worried she was going to burst into tears. Days? Her mother had never used the word 'days' before. She didn't want to lose her brother, but she knew that she was going to.

Parker felt terrible for Madison; she could see the absolute devastation on her face. But at the same time, Parker felt a small joy — Madison had called her a 'friend'.

CHAPTER TWENTY-THREE: MADISON & BEAU

Very little schoolwork was done on Monday. A huge assembly was called in the morning; the students gathered in the quadrangle and were addressed by the principal, Mrs Arndell. She could hear weeping as she delivered the hardest speech she would ever have to give. Mrs Ling and the students would be missed and she, like the students, was devastated. Counsellors were available to all throughout the day and would be visiting classes to talk about the grieving process. The police were also out in force and wanting to interview people.

Class was silent in Mrs Ling's History room. Baldy Baxter stood before the class, in the same spot Mrs Ling stood only days before. He was offering the class a chance to verbalise their feelings, but there were no takers. No one could truly believe what had happened, and talk seemed the last thing they wanted to do. Even Mr Baxter seemed lost for words as he talked about the unusual friendship he shared with Mrs Ling.

Halfway through the class, the police entered the room. They were led by a sharply dressed detective with two uniformed officers. Jeremy grimaced when he saw Madison and Parker in the class; they'd almost had him sent back to his own station with his tail between his legs. He was sure they knew more than they were letting on. He just didn't know how to get it out of them without losing his job.

The detective, Diego Lopez, was tired. He'd barely left the school since Thursday night, and every interview so far had wielded the same results: shock, fear and grief, all mixed with the student's inability to see anything happen around them. Diego nonchalantly pointed at the next group of students he wanted to interview.

Parker stared intently at Henry as he stood; he caught her glare and turned away embarrassed. He still couldn't believe he cried in front of her. He also knew if he hadn't followed her from the backstage area, he probably would have been burnt alive. He refused to believe someone so unpopular could be cleverer than him.

Grayson made some lame joke as he stood, but he could barely muster a few chuckles from a room not ready to laugh.

'Too soon,' muttered one girl.

Amy and Amie also stood.

Amie practised in her head: *just say you were inside and saw nothing*.

Madison was the only one who didn't stand. Diego asked her directly to rise, his patience running short.

'I'm sorry, detective, but I'm sure that Senior Constable Hill will tell you I've already been interviewed and there's no need to question me again.'

The now peeved Diego turned to Jeremy, who could only stammer out that Madison was covered.

Diego muttered, 'Whatever', under his breath and exited.

Jeremy stood defiantly a moment longer, staring at Madison, who simply stared back. He was even more focused on finding out what she knew. As he turned to leave, he caught a glimpse of Parker sitting between Kyle and Griffin. Parker caught his gaze and quickly turned away embarrassed. He knew his instincts were right.

At lunch, Jeremy was determined to find Tina. He thought she was also hiding something, but he couldn't fathom what the three very different females could have in common. After a long search, he finally found her sitting alone in Mrs Ling's History room; he noticed she'd been crying.

She quickly wiped the tears from her eyes and smiled, a smile that hid none of her pain.

'Were you close with Gina Ling?' asked Jeremy. He could never stand to see someone cry.

'No. She didn't really think much of me, and if I'm honest, I didn't like her at all. Isn't that terrible?'

'It's best to be honest, no matter how hard it seems. It's the only thing that helps you get to sleep at night.' Jeremy placed a supporting hand on Tina's shoulder.

'I guess you're not just talking about Gina here?' Tina smiled again at Jeremy. If he wasn't so handsome, she would have pulled her shoulder away. But just because she felt a slight attraction didn't mean she was going to reveal her secret.

'I know you didn't tell me everything, and neither did Parker or Madison. What happened in that shop, and why does it seem to be following you around?' Jeremy looked squarely at Tina.

The pair were sharing a moment, and Tina still hadn't answered.

Soon enough the bell rang, and Tina grinned. 'I have class, and you have it all wrong.' She stood, gently placing her hand on Jeremy, her grin growing bigger. Then she was gone, lost in the sea of students making their way to class.

Jeremy was beguiled.

Tina had managed to catch Parker on her way out the gate after school. She warned Parker that Senior Constable Hill was not giving up. He seemed to be everywhere around the school, so they quickly separated, Tina promising to only be a phone call away.

On the way home, Parker used her secret phone to ask Madison to come to her place, and within five minutes of her arrival home, Madison was there.

'Do you think that if we concentrate hard enough, our lightning bolt could give him amnesia?' Parker gave Madison a dirty look.

'What? Maybe we could, we broke open those doors without causing another fire. Who knows what our powers can really do?'

'It's going to take more than our powers to get rid of him. And who the hell set the hall alight? Do you think it could be Henry?'

After laughing for a few minutes while Parker impatiently waited for her to finish, Madison disagreed with her suspicion of Henry. He was a jerk, but he couldn't set the school on fire. Plus, Madison knew that he'd only been outside selling alcohol. Still, Parker was not convinced.

The pair continued to talk; the conversation seemed to flow easily between them now. They talked over other suspects and what to say when the police hit them up again. Parker even asked about Lachlan.

Fighting back tears, Madison reflected on the day they heard he was sick, the day they heard it had returned, and even worse, the day they were told he would die. Madison broke down in tears, and Parker hugged her for dear life — the glow the only thing seeming to ease Madison's tears. She also felt relief, getting it off her chest; she had held it so close that it was beginning to eat away at her. Now that Parker knew her two greatest secrets, she could no longer pretend Parker wasn't her friend, probably her closest friend.

But Parker already had a best friend, Beau, and he was arriving. Parker heard the bell ring and her mother fussing over Beau, as she always did. She'd always wanted Parker and Beau to get together, something that was clearly never going to happen. Parker had snuck Madison in the back door, as she hadn't needed any more questions from her mother. And now with Beau quickly approaching her room, she had only one option: shove a complaining Madison into her already crowded bedroom closet. Madison was very cramped, with barely an inch to move.

With only seconds to spare, Beau entered.

He didn't notice the guilty look on Parker's face, or the sweat that dripped from her forehead, he was too excited. 'Okay, I may just totally be overacting and seeing things that aren't there, but I'm positive that there's something there.'

Parker was confused. 'What are you talking about?'

'Xavier. I bumped into him down at the shops. He came rushing over to me and told me he was so glad I'd gotten out okay. Said he was worried about me in the fire. I'm not just being like all those silly girls at school, right? I'm sure he likes me.'

Parker's head dropped. She loved that Beau was excited and chose her to share it with; she just wished they were alone.

Madison was straining to hear, and she couldn't believe her ears. She was so caught up in the moment that she tumbled from the closest, dropping to the floor in front of Parker and a very shocked Beau.

'What the hell is she doing here?' asked an embarrassed Beau.

Parker didn't quite know what to say. 'I can explain, I can.'

Beau was confused and desperate to know why Madison was hiding in Parker's room, but more than anything, he was concerned Madison would soon be spreading his greatest secret throughout the school. 'I don't understand,' was all he could say.

'Looks like we've both been hiding in the closet.' Madison couldn't help making a small joke, but the reaction of both Beau and Parker made her realise maybe now wasn't the best time.

Beau's emotions started to build, and tears began to well in his eyes. He didn't want to cry, but his emotions seemed to be taking control. 'Parker, she's going to tell everyone. Every bully in the school is going to come after me.'

'No, Beau, I promise I won't,' Madison said. 'I think it's great; Xavier is hot as, go for it. Please, your secret is safe with me. Parker can tell you how good with secrets I am.' Madison realised Beau was right. While most would be fine with Beau's sexuality, many of the boys at school were clueless Neanderthals who would love to make his life hell.

'She's solid, Beau, she won't tell anyone. You might think it strange, but I trust Madison.' Parker wanted to assure her friend that it was going to be all right. She felt terrible, and her mind was completely on him. This was why she placed a hand on Madison's shoulder, to prove her point. She forgot their emotions were heightened and their powers were constantly getting stronger.

Beau's eyes dried up and his mouth dropped when he suddenly saw a beautiful blue glow between Parker and Madison. The light began to dance between the pair and started to spark in a mini fireworks display. 'What the hell is happening?'

CHAPTER TWENTY-FOUR: DEVON

Mel's parents were concerned. She had locked herself in her room and didn't want to come out. She wasn't eating and claimed she was too sick to attend school. Her parents thought the fire was the reason for their daughter's depression; they just had no idea that she had caused the blaze. They booked an appointment with their local doctor and continued to regularly check that she was okay; they didn't know what else to do.

Devon turned up several times and tried to enter through the window, but Mel locked it, and every time he knocked, she took refuge under the covers of her bed. For all the time she spent in bed, Mel barely slept a wink. Every time she closed her eyes, she could see the flames engulfing the hall, and she could hear the screams of panic. She also kept replaying the moment in her head when she heard that people died in the inferno. The boys told her everyone would escape, but they had blocked the fire doors, and again they all had blood on their hands.

The twins knew something had to be done with the girls.

Amie freaked out at first, accusing the boys of wanting a huge body count from the fire, but Arlo pacified her, and he knew with a little convincing she would do whatever he wanted. Amie was madly in love with Arlo, and he would be able to use that anytime he saw fit.

Mel was another story. She could jeopardise everything, and Arlo was not going to stand for it, no matter how much his brother said he cared for her.

Mel's phone was buzzing all day; she'd left it on silent and didn't want to check any messages. It wasn't till later in the night she finally flicked through her texts. Both Parker and Beau sent several messages, neither had heard from her, and when she didn't come to school, they were worried. This gave Mel some peace; she missed the time she used to spend with them and hoped she may be able to be their number three again soon.

There were also messages from Devon. There was pleading, there were declarations of love, but all the messages contained the one thread — how much he missed her. Mel felt a longing for her boyfriend, but she was also frightened by what he could make her do. In her confusion, Mel knew she could only make one decision right now: she couldn't see Devon until she worked out how she was feeling.

The final text on her phone was from Arlo, and she shuddered as soon as she saw his name. The thought of Arlo put the fear of God into her. Mel saw the look on Arlo's face as the flames began to tear apart the hall, and all she could see was sheer pleasure. She wanted to delete the text immediately, but she had to know what he'd said, even though she knew the message would be nothing but trouble. She opened the message while holding her breath, tears again appeared as she read the words:

Get to the park tonight at midnight or your house will end up just like the school hall.

Mel had to rush to make it to the park. Every part of her wanted to turn and run back home, but she knew Arlo's threat was real. He would light that fire, and he would probably do it while her parents were asleep inside. He'd probably barricade the doors and enjoy the screams when they couldn't get out. Mel knew Arlo would always have the upper hand, and it made her die a little inside.

Full of trepidation, Mel stepped into the park. She could see a dark-blue haze in the distance as she stepped closer. There they stood, defiantly as always. Amie hung off Arlo, the glow emanating from the pair. Mel wondered how Amie could stand being that close to a murderer? She hadn't known that Amie had questioned herself at length, but her affection for Arlo had won out. She forgave him after he promised not to do anything so dangerous again. Both knew he was lying.

Devon stood in anticipation, a large bunch of red roses in his hands. He'd showered, shampooed and shaved. He was wearing aftershave and a new shirt. His father had laughed at him through his drunken haze, but Devon didn't care, he wanted to impress his lady. He rushed forward to greet her, threw his arms around her, and he felt her tense up.

Arlo moved forward, dropping Amie's arm. He was shocked.

As his brother hugged Mel, there was no blue electricity pulsing between the pair — this had never happened before.

Was Mel able to control her powers now? Arlo wondered. Whatever was going on, he was just relieved Mel hadn't noticed.

'I'm sorry, baby, I really am!' Devon meant every word; he didn't want Mel to be upset. He needed her to understand that he was always going to stand by her, but he was also going to follow whatever his brother wanted.

Mel had always secretly feared no man would ever want her. All the girls at her school were getting boyfriends, and no boy ever looked sideways at her, except for Warwick Puck, but there was no chance of her going for a guy known for his flatulence issues. She feared she'd go through high school without ever being kissed. So having a boy as hot as Devon be in love with her should have been a dream come true — it was anything but.

Mel couldn't talk to Devon, and she pulled away. His face displaying his hurt. Amie rolled her eyes, making sure that Mel saw her disgust.

Arlo was the only one to remain stoic. He was the leader, and he knew it. It was time for him to take control. 'Mel, let's go for a walk.'

Before fear could even take hold of Mel, Devon voiced his concerns. He had been upset when he heard his twin's threat to burn her house and didn't want his brother to threaten her anymore.

But Arlo replied, 'Don't worry, bro; I'll look after your girl. I promise.'

So off they went, leaving Devon and Amie waiting in silence.

Mel's walk was stilted; inside she was stopping herself from turning and running.

Arlo was calm; he knew what he had to do. He stopped far enough away so that he was still visible to his brother and his girlfriend — they could see Mel and Arlo but not hear what Arlo had to say. He stood facing the others, mainly so they couldn't see Mel's face as he laid it on the line for her. 'There has to be a reason why out of everyone in this world you are the match for my brother. And that's not the only reason he likes you. He seems to really think he loves you.'

Mel was surprised by his candour. She'd never seen this

side of Arlo, and it might not have changed much, but she would no longer think him stupid.

'The thing is, Mel, you should consider yourself lucky. You really have no friends. Even the dork and gay kid don't want you hanging around them anymore. They've already replaced you with that new kid and the other loser no one likes.'

Mel immediately regretted briefly letting down her guard. She should have known what Arlo was like — the nastiest person she'd ever met.

'And we've taken you in, made you one of us. My brother wants to be with you, even though you're not that pretty.'

At that moment it was fortunate for Arlo that Devon couldn't see his girlfriend's face, because the tears she'd been shedding for days flowed again. 'Why would you say that?' asked Mel, tasting the bitterness of her tears. Arlo was saying everything she had always feared.

'I'm not trying to make you cry. You got chosen to be with us, and we both need to learn to deal with that. The only thing we know for sure is that we gotta stick together; we're family now.' Arlo was not usually big on words; he only said what he felt he needed to.

'Okay, so I'm ugly and you need me. What? To kill more people? Cause I won't, and if that means I end up completely alone, so be it.'

Arlo knew the buttons to push. He knew how unattractive and unpopular Mel felt, and he knew he could use that against her and to control her. 'I promise, no more hurting people.'

Mel believed him. She shook his hand and ran to hug her boyfriend, the dark-blue sparks returning as they embraced and kissed. Her relationship with Devon meant too much, and she couldn't walk away from that, no matter how bad a person that made her.

Arlo casually walked back to the group, a smirk hiding in the corner of his mouth. He'd totally played Mel. If he wanted to hurt someone, he was going to. No one was going to stop him — after all, he was a God.

CHAPTER TWENTY-FIVE: KYLE & PARKER

Every Tuesday afternoon, Kyle's grandmother played lawn bowls. It was the highlight of her week, and when Kyle moved to Sydney to be with her, she told him she would give it up to be home when he arrived back from school. Kyle assured her he was certainly old enough to look after himself one afternoon a week. And today, an empty house was just what he and his friends needed.

As expected, Beau had a million and one questions about the light he saw. Madison at first tried to make up all kinds of wild stories about science experiments and freak lightning strikes in the Bennett house, but Beau wasn't buying any of it. It wasn't because of Beau's sharp intellect; this had everything to do with his ability to read his best friend's face.

They only silenced Beau when they promised him an answer the following day.

And that Tuesday was hell for Parker, as Beau's questions were incessant. But she remained firm; all questions would be answered that afternoon.

Parker and Beau were whispering so much all day it made Mel feel completely rejected, and Arlo's words rattled around her head — especially after Beau went to the canteen and Parker began whispering to both Griffin and Kyle.

The day dragged on for Beau, and with double Math to finish the day, he thought the end of school would never come. There was an extra spring in his step as he followed Kyle, Parker and Griffin to Kyle's house. He had no idea why the others were coming, but he didn't care, he knew this was going to be big, and he was ready to learn all.

Drinks were served, as was the cake Kyle's grandmother kindly baked when she heard he was having guests. Small talk was non-existent while they all waited for Madison to arrive.

Soon enough the doorbell rang and the five sat around in the antique lounge room. Kyle's grandmother was a collector. She had wooden maps of Australia hanging all over her walls, all filled with teaspoons from every square inch of Australia. Pride of place was an old black and white framed photo of her husband in his army outfit, with his bravery medals displayed proudly next to it.

'All right, guys, I'm ready to jump out of my skin! What the hell is going on?' asked an excited Beau.

Madison said she didn't want another person to know, especially someone who didn't share their ability. Griffin and Kyle agreed with her — the more who knew, the more chance they could be outed. But Beau knew about secrets, and Parker knew she could trust him with her life, so this secret would be simple.

Parker began to explain the story: the convenience store, the staff toilets, Kyle's first day. There was the flip side. The ATMs, the school disco, Mrs Ling. Parker left no stone unturned. She was ready for Beau to suddenly rise at any moment, call her the worst friend for keeping this secret and then storm out, never to return.

Instead, he sat like a child on Christmas morning, unsure

which present to open next. He tore through the stories, constantly asking for details. Beau was a film buff, and his favourite genre was the superhero flick — it now felt like he'd been cast in one. 'I have to see a demonstration!'

There seemed little reason to argue; they'd already told him everything, and he seemed more elated than any of them ever were. Plus, they knew the pain Parker went through not telling him. Soon they were standing with their hands ready to join. As they grew closer, sparks began to fly between them and all around them, and all four glowed a beautiful soft blue.

Beau happily sat awestruck.

When the four finally joined hands, a blue lightning bolt circled frantically around the group. Beau let out a squeal of delight, 'This is the best thing I've ever seen.'

At first, they were hesitant around Beau, but his enthusiasm was contagious. They all loved showing an outsider what they could do; they'd almost become blasé by the wonder of their abilities. Soon they were showing Beau tricks, and the five were having the best afternoon they'd had in ages.

'But where did it come from?'

'We don't know, we honestly don't,' answered Parker. Her powers were an enigma to her.

'It would drive me crazy not knowing. Superman knew he was from Krypton, Spiderman knew he'd been bitten, and the Hulk, well, we all know how that happened.' Beau smiled at Madison — she had no idea what he was talking about. 'You've got to know your origins so you can understand your powers.' Beau was overjoyed — this was a dream come true for him.

'But we're not superheroes,' Kyle was quick to add in.

'Are you sure? Didn't you save a heap of people at the school disco with your powers? That's classic superhero stuff!'

The room suddenly went quiet, everyone lost in their own thoughts. Beau's points had merit, and they couldn't help but fantasise a little. Madison was even visualising herself in a cute little outfit; it would have to be pink.

'So ... I'm guessing none of you have been exposed to nuclear waste? Or been hit by lightning recently? It can't be something too obvious or you would have worked it out before,' spoke Beau wisely.

It quickly became apparent that telling Beau could have been a blessing in disguise. While many of his comments were based on films, he was also making valid points, and after knowing their secret for a short time, he was determined to find out more. He wanted to be the key to discovering the secret of their powers.

Beau had his laptop out and was quickly building a spreadsheet to compare what the four had in common. It seemed difficult and a little hopeless at first, especially since Kyle's powers emerged when he was in a completely different state. Then after a long interrogation of all in the room, Beau found a similarity they all shared. 'You were all born within four days of each other at the exact same hospital. Now, that can't be a coincidence.'

They realised that he was right.

Kyle was born on June 30th, Parker July 1st, Madison had been born on the 2nd, while Griffin celebrated his birthday on July 3rd. Could they have had their powers for this long?

The afternoon began with an enthralled Beau soaking in all the details he could and finished with the four of them hanging off Beau's every word. He was throwing out theories, and they were intrigued. They could have sat all afternoon pitching ideas, but Madison's phone rang: it was Grayson.

'Where are you, babe? I feel like I never get to see you anymore.'

Madison tried to delay him and make an excuse.

But Grayson wasn't used to rejection and was beginning to act petulant. He informed Madison that he was on his way over and that she had to be there when he arrived.

She wanted to yell at him, she wanted to tell him she was doing something more important than making out, but she couldn't. She couldn't risk him finding out what was happening.

With Madison's departure, it seemed the appropriate time to finish for the day. Plus, Beau was keen to talk to his neighbour who worked in the administration at the hospital they were all born in. He could see himself rifling through hospital records to find the secret. Beau wished he had powers, but for now he was happy to cement his position in the team with his intellect.

Madison left with Beau, the pair chatting happily about his theories and his plan to be a super sleuth. Griffin followed behind; he found Beau amusing and was intrigued to hear more ideas. Parker politely thanked Kyle and was ready to head off with the others.

'Parker, please, can you stay for a minute?'

The door closed and the others were gone, leaving Parker and Kyle alone. The first time they'd been alone since they almost kissed.

Kyle had tried to talk to Parker several times since then, but he could never get her alone. He hadn't been able to stop thinking about Parker. Mostly, though, he hated that she may suspect he had ulterior motives for their relationship. 'We never got to finish the conversation we started.'

'Too much has happened, and I'm not angry. I know why you came looking for me, and you were right, we do share a power. We should be happy about that.' Parker was deflecting; she didn't want to talk about her non-existent love life.

'Please, Parker. Yeah, one of the reasons I came here was to find you and to find out why your photo helped me.' Kyle paused, becoming emotional. 'And then when I found you, I could never have imagined how great you'd be.'

'You don't have to say that; you're one of us now.' Parker had managed to convince herself Kyle was merely interested in her for her powers. She thought she was crazy for ever thinking that a boy as good-looking as Kyle could be interested in her.

'But I want more than that. I want to be your boyfriend.' Kyle smiled, a small blue glow seeming to radiate from his mouth.

'Why?' asked Parker, and the glow disappeared. 'I reckon you could have any girl in our school, so why would you want me?'

'Because you don't know how special you are. You're the most fascinating person I've ever met. You're smart, you're witty, you're honest. And you're beautiful.' As Kyle spoke, the glow returned — a beautiful blue light grew from deep within him.

Parker listened to his words and watched the light build, and she knew he meant them. A single blue tear fell from her eye and slowly worked its way down her face.

Kyle put his hand forward to wipe away the tear. As he touched her face, his fingers began to spark. The little bolts of electricity jumped from his fingertips into Parker's skin. And instead of jolting her, they soothed and healed her hurt and doubt.

Kyle leaned towards her, and Parker closed her eyes as she gently moved her head forward. Kyle tenderly kissed her lips, and Parker felt like she was floating. Both had never experienced a kiss before and could imagine nothing else being this perfect. The room filled with blue light, and electricity danced around the pair as they continued to kiss.

CHAPTER TWENTY-SIX: GRAYSON

Grayson was not happy. Madison was full of personality; it was one of the reasons he liked her. He enjoyed the little power struggles they partook in, but he was getting restless. They'd practically been together for two years, and he thought it was time for the relationship to take the next step. He always thought Madison felt the same way, that was until recently. Madison was pulling away, and Grayson was convinced she was seeing someone else.

Grayson phoned from outside Madison's house. He knew she wasn't home; her big dog Britney was roaming around the backyard. When Madison was home, Britney was usually by her side. He decided to set a trap, so when he phoned to demand she come home, he hid in the garden across the road. He wanted to see if Madison was going to be dropped home in a car, or on a motorbike. He imagined the only guy who could lure Madison away from him would be a university student, or a biker, maybe even a uni student biker.

It only took fifteen minutes before the beautiful Madison walked towards her front door. Grayson couldn't believe his eyes — instead of the ripped older guy he was picturing, she was walking with Beau. *Beau? How could she cheat with him?* Then to really rub salt into the wound, they were chatting happily ... and Madison was laughing. Not the polite laugh she offered whenever Grayson attempted humour, but a full-bellied laugh.

Grayson watched as the pair said goodbye with a long hug, but he wasn't going to just sit there waiting to see if they kissed, that would be too much for him. 'Get your dirty hands off my girlfriend,' he shouted as he stormed towards the pair.

Beau was terrified! Grayson was bigger than him, stronger than him and usually fond of calling him names. This was not going to end well.

'Grayson, what are you doing? Were you spying on me?' yelled Madison. She was annoyed. She knew Grayson was getting clingy, but this was ridiculous. For the first time, she was questioning whether her greatly detailed wedding was even going to be with Grayson.

'I can't believe you'd cheat on me with this guy. I hate this guy.' Grayson's anger was reaching boiling point. With all his frustration and force, Grayson shoved Beau. The intensity was so fierce it knocked Beau straight onto the concrete foot path, leaving his elbow and palm a bloody mess.

Beau tried to control his emotions — he wanted to cry, he wanted to run — but stayed frozen in fear.

'Grayson, you moron, don't touch him.' Madison was horrified by Grayson's actions. Her father had always called Grayson an idiot, and for the first time she could see it. She felt terrible for poor Beau; she could see how terrified he was. 'Nothing is going on with Beau and I, we're just friends.'

'We're not friends with THESE people; he's a loser,' responded Grayson as he picked up Beau by the throat, making him squirm in agony. 'And you were hugging him, you were about to kiss him.' Grayson made a fist with his other hand and lined up his punch, ready to knock some teeth from Beau's mouth.

Beau tried to scream, but nothing came out, he was too scared.

Madison tried to pull Grayson away, but he was too strong, and nothing was going to stop him from attacking the petrified Beau. Madison was so panicked, she just screamed without thinking, 'He's gay.'

Grayson dropped Beau from his grasp, Beau falling onto the concrete again. Grayson was unsure what to think at first. He'd long suspected Beau was gay; he'd been a popular target for the passing insult. But Grayson saw him hug his girlfriend, and she'd been lying about where she'd been. Then Grayson looked at Beau's face. He saw the fear and knew Madison was telling the truth. Beau was gay, and Grayson planned on telling everyone at school the next day.

After the panic momentarily subsided, Beau gained the courage to run. He was up before anyone realised, and he sprinted the three blocks home.

Grayson called out some nasty taunts as Beau took off. When he turned around, his face locked in a grin, ready to kiss his girlfriend, but she was already heading off inside. 'Wait for me, babe,' he said.

'No, Grayson, that was mean. You can go home; I won't be seeing you today.' And with that, Madison slammed the front door.

Grayson was left standing alone. He was angry, and he knew someone would pay tomorrow, and that person would be Beau.

Parker barely registered the television news the next morning, she was still on cloud nine. Her parents were concerned about another local ATM explosion. Police were worried that the skill of the bandits had evolved, and they were still no closer to finding out who the culprits were. Parker also didn't notice her brother as he annoyingly buzzed around the kitchen complaining about another diet his mother was imposing.

She beamed as she stepped from her front door where Kyle was waiting for her, wearing a similar grin. They both wanted to run and hug each other, plant a million kisses on each other's lips, but they knew they couldn't touch. As it was, they really had to concentrate to contain their powers on the way to school, because just being in the same vicinity was giving them an occasional blue tinge.

The pair walked to school, smiling the whole way. They didn't notice the buzz that circulated through the school grounds as they entered. Parker was desperate to see Beau. She had tried to call him multiple times last night and this morning, but his phone kept ringing out and he answered no texts. She now saw him sitting with Griffin and Mel and raced across, ready to share her amazing news with them. However, she instantly knew Beau was not in the mood for stories of her love life.

Beau sat with his head in his hands, his face stained with tears. His uniform was stained, partially in grass and partially with food. He'd been pushed down by a group of students who threw their lunch at him. If a teacher hadn't been close by, Beau had worried about what else the students would have done.

'What's happened?' asked Parker.

Beau couldn't talk; it'd taken Griffin and Mel fifteen minutes to get Beau to give away the small details he had. It was left to Griffin to explain what the drama was. 'Madison accidentally let it slip to Grayson that Beau was gay, and Grayson's told everyone. It hasn't been a good start to the day for Beau.'

Parker was furious. She wanted to grab Kyle and shoot a lightning bolt straight into Grayson, and maybe even give Madison a quick burn for her trouble. 'Why would Madison tell him?'

Beau looked up and spoke for the first time, his eyes bloodshot. 'Grayson was trying to beat me up, and it slipped out. I don't blame her.'

'Well, I do. She'll be getting a piece of mind when I see her! We trusted her,' countered Parker — no one messed with her best friend.

Before Beau could argue, Mel chimed in, utterly confused. 'Why did you tell Madison you were gay, you never told me? I thought I was your second best friend?'

'It's not like that, Mel, I didn't tell her on purpose. She was at Parker's, and she overheard. She was the only other one to know until today.' Beau was starting to feel better being surrounded by his support network.

'Why was Madison at your house? It feels like you haven't invited me over for ages. Two weeks ago, you didn't speak to Griffin, and now he's a regular at your house, and two weeks ago you didn't even know Kyle. Now everyone, including people who you've never liked, gets an invite around, but I never do.' Arlo's statements had been rattling around her head, and the time bomb was about to detonate.

'You don't need an invite to my house, you're welcome anytime,' responded Parker, surprised. She'd never heard Mel raise her voice before, and now she was practically screaming at her.

'Well, it doesn't feel like that, especially with all the whispering and stuff going on. Arlo was right; you guys don't even want me hanging around.'

'Arlo?' asked Parker. *Why is Mel talking to Arlo? We once had a conversation about how terrifying he is. Why is*

Mel talking to Arlo about our group? Before Parker could ask any of these questions, or even get an answer for the first question, Mel was off. She scooped up her bag and was storming across the quadrangle, ignoring the calls from Parker and Beau to come back.

'What just happened?' asked Parker to her friends, who were equally as confused.

Parker searched for Mel throughout the day, and when she tried to call her, Mel's phone was off. So, she guessed Mel had gone home. She had no idea why Mel exploded, and she felt bad because she didn't really have the time today to look after Mel's ego; she had to protect Beau. Maybe Mel was right after all?

Beau received more than his usual number of taunts that day, all of them unimaginative. Parker argued back as often as she could, while Beau just kept his head down. He kept wondering if Xavier had heard and what his response would be.

Madison avoided them all day, horribly embarrassed by what had happened.

Amy came to talk to Beau and hugged him tightly. She was happy for him, even though she admitted she'd hoped for more with him.

Beau couldn't help but like her, for he knew he'd found a good friend. He had other students come to wish him well and say they were happy for him. Liane Singh, a Year 11 girl who'd recently come out, came to welcome him 'to the club'. This gave Beau a slight hope that he would be okay.

However, the day dragged on for Beau, and he was glad when he was finally walking home. Parker offered him a chance to take refuge at her house, but Beau knew he had to go home and talk to his mum before she heard the story on the grapevine. He was nervous, but hopeful that she would support him.

Beau was only a block from home, preparing his confession for his mum. He was so caught up in his preparation that he didn't see Grayson, Henry and Clark approaching him. When he finally saw them, they were too close for him to run, and he knew he could never outrun Henry. He wanted to say something, reason with them, but words seemed to fail him. He knew what was coming.

The three called Beau every insult they could, Grayson leading the charge. Soon they were circling around him, shoving him as they paced. The three beamed with pride; they enjoyed picking on the weaker kids, as it always made them feel stronger.

Beau stood frozen, waiting for the worst to begin.

And begin it did ... Soon the names and the shoving became more ferocious. The boys were whipping each other into a frenzy. They had all felt they'd had their self-worth taken from them recently, and they were trying to claim it back in whatever means possible. Their fragile masculinity had been threatened, and violence was their way to regain strength.

Before long, Beau was on the grass after being hit by Grayson, and all three were ferociously kicking him. Beau tried to cover himself, but it seemed futile, their kicks were everywhere. The names flowed along with the kicks, as did the laughs.

Beau could feel himself losing consciousness and tasted blood in his mouth. Luckily, he was saved by an old lady with a broom who came rushing out of her house, ready to whack the boys across the head. At first, they swore at her and told her to mind her own business, but after she informed them that she'd called the police, the three sprinted off, high-fiving as they went.

Parker rushed to the hospital as soon as she heard what

happened. Beau had several broken ribs, and the doctors said he was lucky the injuries weren't more serious. He was heavily sedated and was still asleep. She sat by his side, tears in her eyes. She spoke to him, apologised for not being there and promised him he'd never be hurt like this again. She even joked to him that he would do anything to get closer to the hospital record room and continue his work to discover the origins of their 'powers'.

The sun set and Parker's parents, while devastated for Beau, thought it was time for Parker to return home. Begrudgingly, Parker kissed Beau's forehead lovingly and exited. Just as she was walking out of the hospital, Madison and Griffin appeared. Both wore their apologises across their face.

As soon as Parker saw Madison heading towards her, her expression was one of disdain. 'Don't even talk to me; your boyfriend is the biggest loser in the world.'

'I'm sorry, Parker, I didn't know he'd act like that,' pleaded Madison.

'You spent all this time wishing you weren't connected to us, "the dorks". You've been so condescending, acting like you were doing us a favour by hanging around us. But you were the lucky one, cause you actually got to see what real friends are like, and you're not one of mine.' Parker was angry, she was upset, and she wanted to take it out on someone — Madison was the easy target.

'What are you saying?' asked Madison, devastated and worried that Parker was right.

'This little thing we have going on, it's over. I don't care if I never use my power again, as long as I don't see you or any of your horrid friends.' Parker didn't wait for an answer; she stormed off, hating herself for letting tears escape.

Madison probably would have cried if she wasn't so shocked.

Griffin felt the words too. This group had become important and meant so much to him. He was no longer a loner, and he had grown to like it. He was not ready for it to end.

'Aren't you going to follow her? Run as far away from me as possible?' asked Madison, feeling sorry for herself.

'No, I don't think you should be alone,' responded Griffin.

'She's so lucky. She has two wonderful guys interested in her. All I have is some bigoted pretty boy who's probably going to get really fat and bald within ten years.' Madison was not used to rejection, and she was beginning to wallow in her own misery.

'Two guys?' quizzed Griffin.

'Kyle, and you,' answered Madison.

'It's not Parker I like,' responded Griffin softly, nervous to say any more.

'But you're always following her around, and you were jealous when Kyle came onto the scene. You didn't make him very welcome at all.'

'Of course I was jealous, I was the only guy, and I was worried about someone new joining us. And as for Parker, she's like a sister to me; I want to make sure she's okay.' Griffin breathed in deeply before speaking again — this was what he'd been wanting to say for so long. And finally, he admitted, 'You're the one I like.'

CHAPTER TWENTY-SEVEN: LACHLAN

Sleep eluded Madison for most of the night. She tossed and turned, her mind full. Parker's rejection played on repeat, and she couldn't believe how much it affected her. She also couldn't stop thinking about Grayson. He was her Prince Charming once, but now she was pretty sure she hated him. When she returned home, she took her very thick wedding folder and threw it in the bin. She'd never seen her father happier. She would go to the police station in the morning and tell them Grayson and his idiotic mates should be charged with assault.

Then there was Griffin. She could have slapped him; she should have laughed at him, but she didn't say anything to him. She wasn't sure how she felt. Things were changing too quickly for her, and she didn't think she was ready.

Sleep finally arrived at 5am; it was mainly due to sheer exhaustion. The last thing she expected were her parents to burst through her door at 6am, her mother in tears. Lachlan was in and out of consciousness, barely able to recognise his surroundings. He was delirious, and her parents were convinced today would be his last one.

Madison jumped from bed and ran to his room. She

cried when she saw him. He was frail and had steadily been losing weight. She kissed his forehead and wept; this was the day she had been fearing for a long very time.

School was the furthest thing from Madison's mind that day, and she was on the absent list along with Beau. Beau was the hot topic in the school yard, many outraged by what had happened to him. Then there were those who were treating Grayson and his cronies as heroes. That was until the police arrived at school, again.

At first it was thought they were there to continue their hopeless investigation into the fire. But when Grayson, Henry and Clark were pulled from class, the buzz in the school was that the boys were busted big time. The old lady with the broom had called the police because she recognised the local boys. With Beau's statement, the boys were going to be charged. They were dragged from the school at recess, Clark crying his eyes out. People began to point and laugh.

When Parker heard what was happening, she rushed across to witness the spectacle for herself. She pushed through the crowd just as the door to the police car was being closed on Grayson. He looked at her, trying to conceal his panic, and he caught the gleam in her eyes. She smiled and clapped; he turned away.

He had gotten carried away and never meant for it to go that far. His parents were going to kill him.

Mel also wasn't at school that day, her phone still off. Beau's phone was running hot because he kept phoning Parker for the latest news, and he was cheered up when he heard of the arrest. Parker and Kyle continued to stand as close together as they could without starting a lightning strike. They were falling in love and were so happy.

Griffin was having a quiet day; he contemplated spending his lunch in the library, alone. He was angry with himself for becoming so involved with everyone, and he wished he'd said nothing to Madison. She had just looked at him and then walked away. As if someone so beautiful would want to be with him. He knew he was better as a loner, and that was what he was destined for.

Doctors came and went from the O'Sullivan residence; it was suggested that they rush Lachlan to hospital, but Madison's parents didn't see the point. He hadn't wanted to go to the hospital before, and this was where he felt most comfortable, in his room, surrounded by his things and his family. Britney planted herself at the base of the bed, her head down. Madison sat beside the bed and spent hours reading to her brother. She tried not to cry as she read his favourite stories. The whole family stayed in the room, waiting, praying for some kind of miracle.

Then at roughly 4pm, Lachlan lost his long battle with leukemia. Madison was holding one of his hands, his mother the other. His father sat at the top of the bed, caressing his son's hair. They listened intently to his laboured breath and listened as that breath ceased. All three broke down in tears, Madison's mother crying uncontrollably. This would be the darkest day the family would ever experience.

The family seemed to sit in the same positions for a very long time, no one wanting to get up or leave brave Lachlan. Finally, Mr O'Sullivan rose. He'd been putting off calling the relevant authorities. Seeing Lachlan taken away would make this all too final and real. He took hold of Madison's mum, scooping her in his arms and from the room. She was inconsolable, and Mr O'Sullivan thought his next call would be to the doctor to sedate his devastated wife.

Madison was left in the room. She lightly stroked her brother's cheeks as she cried. She couldn't accept this was the end. She could not let her brother die at the age of eleven, it just wasn't right.

Parker and Kyle were alone in her bedroom. They lay on the floor, talking and stealing kisses. Parker was waiting for her phone to ring. Beau was being released from hospital and promised to phone the moment he arrived home; she needed to be by his side. He had also finally spoken to his mum in the hospital about the reason for his beating. She was upset at first, and quiet, but eventually she said that she had suspected he would someday come out. She would be fine; she would just need some time. Beau knew for now that was enough. Parker was ready to come to the rescue and entertain her dearest friend, taking his mind off his dramas.

Her mobile rang and she jumped to answer it. She stopped dead in her tracks though when she saw Madison's pseudonym on her screen. She had turned off the secret phone and buried it in the bottom of her junk drawer — she didn't want to hear from Madison ever again. She couldn't believe Madison would now break her own rules and call on her actual mobile.

Within seconds, Parker's home phone rang, and she could hear her mother walking towards her room. Kyle jumped up and sat himself nervously on Parker's computer chair. Being in a couple was new to him, and he didn't want Mrs Bennett to think anything inappropriate was going on.

Julia soon entered the room, phone in hand. She didn't bother knocking, almost hoping to bust her daughter in a compromising position. She forgave Parker for past indiscretions and was delighted her daughter had found a nice boyfriend, the son of an old friend. She smiled when she saw Kyle sitting nervously. 'Madison O'Sullivan's on the phone for you. Are you two friends now?'

'No,' was Parker's quick response. 'You can tell her I'm not home.'

'You can tell her yourself, because I'm not lying for you.' Julia threw down the phone and exited the room. Her daughter's seemingly new-found popularity was strange to her, and she was interested to find out more, but she was also unwilling to become involved in teenage politics.

Parker felt like hanging the phone straight up, but she thought Madison was tenacious enough to ring back. Instead, she settled on giving her another piece of her mind. 'Listen Madison, I thought I told you yesterday that I didn't want anything to do with you anymore.'

There was a pause, and Parker wasn't sure if Madison was even on the other end of the receiver.

Finally, a meek and teary voice spoke in a hushed voice, 'Please, Parker, you have to come over now. It's my brother.'

Parker ran as fast as she could to Madison's house. Kyle offered to join her, but she knew this was just between the two of them. It didn't matter how angry she was with her, this was about Lachlan, and she knew how much he suffered.

Breathless, Parker was at Madison's front door within minutes and was secretly being ushered in the door and into Lachlan's room by Madison. Parker stopped in shock when she saw him lying peacefully in his bed. She hadn't seen him in a long time and was stunned to see him so thin and frail. 'Is he okay?' she asked softly.

'No,' came Madison's hushed response, 'he died an hour ago.'

Parker placed a supportive hand on Madison's shoulder and apologised with all her heart. A soft blue light glowed between the pair, and blue electricity seemed to radiate from Parker, into Madison. 'We have to try and bring him back,' stated Madison with all the determination in the world.

A confused Parker asked, 'How'?

'What good are powers if we can't use them to save people? To save my brother?'

Parker thought Madison had a point. They hadn't discovered the extent of their abilities, so maybe this was something they could do. At least, they had to try it. There was no possible way Parker could say no to a devastated Madison.

Madison led Parker closer to Lachlan's bed. A breeze lazily entered through the open window, and Britney still laid guard at the base of the bed. She gently lifted her head to look at Parker, but then the large dog dropped her head again, mourning the loss of her dear friend.

Parker and Madison joined hands, the blue light dancing around their grasp. They placed their hands slowly on Lachlan's forehead, which was turning cold. Madison's tears turned a blue colour as the pair tried their best to help him. The electricity surged between the pair, generating voracity, but it didn't seem to have an effect on Lachlan. The electricity did not even seem to touch his pale skin.

'We have to try harder. I can't let him die.'

Madison was getting frustrated, and Parker wished more than anything that their powers would bring him back to life, but it seemed futile. She lifted her hands; they'd left a small mark on Lachlan's forehead. 'Madison, it's not working. He's gone.'

Madison was getting angry. 'No, I won't let him be dead. We can do this; we have to do this.' Madison grabbed hold of Parker's hands again, this time quite ferociously, forcing them back onto her brother's head. 'Now concentrate, really hard. Please.'

Madison begged, and Parker's heart shattered. Her own brother drove her crazy, but she would be destroyed if she lost him. Parker tried to dig deep, with all her might, trying to bring Lachlan back to life. The blue light grew stronger between the pair, now filling the room. Britney cowered in the corner. But still the light didn't seep into Lachlan.

Madison was an emotional wreck as she tried to save her

brother. Tears flooded from her eyes. A beautiful blue tear drop fell from her eyes, landed on their hands and dribbled down on to Lachlan's face. From this single blue drop, the blue light slowly started to be absorbed by Lachlan's skin, and he began to radiate a glorious blue.

'It's working,' shouted Madison.

Parker filled with pride, and the pair continued attempting to soak their powers into Lachlan. Finally, as the blue light reached Lachlan's toes, covering all his body, there was a loud crash. Lachlan's bedroom window exploded, and a mirror shattered. Electricity fields and lightning bolts were dancing around the room, and the girls were thrown to the floor.

Madison's parents sprinted into the room, bursting through the door. Britney almost knocked them over, running from the room to hide. Her parents were ready to yell and scream, but they were stopped dead in their tracks.

Madison and Parker were both slowly getting up, dazed. The room was a disaster area: furniture overturned and everything trashed. The only thing that stayed in immaculate condition was Lachlan's bed.

Then, there was Lachlan. He was now sitting up in his bed. The colour had returned to his body, as did the smile they hadn't seen in such a long time. It was a complete miracle, Lachlan was alive.

CHAPTER TWENTY-EIGHT: TINA & BEAU

Lachlan was raced straight to hospital, but he was hungry and would rather have gone to McDonalds. He hadn't had or felt like junk food in ages, and now he craved it. The doctors ran all the tests they could, prodding and poking Lachlan, but nothing. The O'Sullivans were stunned to hear that not only was Lachlan in fine health, but he was now also completely cancer free.

Doctors came from everywhere to see the medical miracle. The O'Sullivans swore he'd died, and their oncologist was telling everyone that when he left Lachlan that morning, Lachlan only had hours left. The ambulance drivers who had arrived on the scene told everyone who would listen about the mayhem in the room and the scorch marks on the wall. Everyone was talking, except the miracle boy's sister, who was unusually silent.

Madison was asked many times what happened, even she was struggling to make up stories. She muttered that it was a freak lightning strike on the house, and it was the story that seemed to be sticking. It seemed highly improbable to those who heard the argument, but with no other theories circulating, it was somehow believed.

Word spread fast, and by the time Madison returned to

school on Monday, it had reached fever pitch. Madison, who once loved her moments in the spotlight, was unusually coy, and that made people even more intrigued. Even Amy and Amie were shocked, for they had no idea Lachlan was ill. Amie's attention was certainly piqued, she had heard something about freak lightning, but her and the twins were too self-absorbed to believe that anyone else could share their power, especially someone as vacuous as Madison.

Two others returned to school that day, Beau and Mel.

Both were also talking points. A heavily bandaged and limping Beau was treated like a hero in many circles, mostly by those who despised Grayson and company. Grayson's reign of terror had been cut short, and even though it took a heavy beating to stop them, Beau was now a hero to many.

Mel, on the other hand, was now the subject of terrible rumours. She arrived at school that day with the Thomas twins, fresh from their suspension. Devon and Mel had practised controlling their powers and were now able to touch without showing their dark-blue light. This meant that they were now able to be affectionate in public, and affectionate they were.

Parker tried to approach Mel, nervously walking over to where she was sitting with the twins. But before she could even reach her old friend, she was ridiculed and called every name under the sun.

'Mel, please come back and sit with us, we miss you,' pleaded Parker, but Mel turned away; Arlo's brainwashing complete.

'Sorry, ugly, she's with us now,' called out Arlo.

Parker left confused. *When and how did this happen? What can Mel possibly be thinking?* Parker was devastated to lose the friendship of someone who just two weeks ago had been one of her only two friends. Things had changed so drastically, mostly good, but this proved to Parker there were two sides to every situation.

That lunch, Tina called her four students to the classroom.

One by one they arrived. Firstly, Madison and Griffin entered the room, smiling nervously at each other. They still hadn't talked since Griffin's startling confession. They were quickly followed by Parker and Kyle, happy to be together again. Beau was the final one to hobble into the room.

Tina was surprised; she wondered why Beau was there and why the others weren't objecting to his presence. 'Ah, Beau, what are you doing here?'

'Well, Tina, they've told me everything and they want me involved in all discussions from here on in.' Beau smiled.

Tina wanted to smack him in the face. 'Tina?' She wasn't sure how she was going to react to Beau being in the room.

'This isn't exactly a school project here. I'd like to think when it comes to their powers, that you and I are peers. So, unless you want to call me Mr Hardigan, I'll call you Tina,' Beau replied. His new-found confidence was at an all-time high. The world knew his greatest secret, and he'd survived, albeit with some broken ribs. Beau was stronger.

Tina wanted to tell Beau where to stick his Mr Hardigan. Mostly, she wanted to throw him from the room, but she knew that he was Parker's best friend, and if she wanted him there, he was staying.

Things were very tense in the room, not just between Tina and Beau. Madison and Griffin were still trying not to look at each other. And even though they saved the life of her brother the day before, Madison and Parker were still not talking. Their group was in shambles.

Tina was curious to know what had happened in Lachlan's room, and for the first time, Madison was able to honestly tell of the miracle that had saved her brother. Tears couldn't help but flow as Madison told the group how she truly believed she'd lost her brother. As she was finishing telling the story, she turned to Parker, her emotions still heightened. 'The thing is, I know that you're still angry with me about Grayson, and I deserve that. I never wanted us to be friends, but I'm so glad that we are. Because even when you were angry with me, you dropped everything and came and saved my brother. That's what a real friend does, so thank you.'

Parker was floored by Madison's honesty. She knew they'd shared something special in Lachlan's room, she just wasn't sure if she could completely trust someone who barely knew her name only weeks ago.

'Parker, you can't be angry with Madison because of me, cause I'm not. And I don't want you to be.' Beau was eager for the group to return to the excitement they shared at Kyle's house when all had been revealed to him. He wanted many more meetings like this, and he wanted to see them use their powers again.

'We were given these powers for a reason. I truly believe that. We did something good with them last night. We can do that again.' Madison beamed at the group, and they couldn't help but be inspired by her.

Griffin was reminded why he felt so strongly for her.

'You're right. I'm sorry about what I said. I do like the friendship we've built, and I would hate to stop using our powers.' Parker was ready to forgive and forget, and more importantly, move forward.

'Good. Friends again. But we don't have to hug, do we?' Madison cheekily grinned, and Parker laughed. This friendship meant more than either would admit.

'I'm glad you've sorted that out because we need you guys unified and ready for the next challenge. What do we think it'll be?' asked Tina.

'I think that one's pretty obvious, Tina,' Beau knew he was annoying her and was enjoying it. He felt she under graded his last essay, and he was ready for revenge. 'You lot have to stop those freaks who burnt down the hall. Did you hear they just hit another ATM?'

Tina fumed! She knew Beau was right, she just wondered whether he needed to be so patronising when he pointed it out. And then she realised it was the same patronising tone he used in his last essay when describing the battle between the Montagues and the Capulets.

'But we have no idea who they are? It couldn't have been Henry; he was still in custody when the last ATM was hit.' Parker's suspicions had been incorrect, and she didn't have any other suspects.

'I had nothing else to do when I was stuck in bed, so I did some research. Took me a while, but I may have lied to get access to get some school records.'

Tina looked at Beau and knew she should be mad, but she wanted to hear what he had to say.

'I looked up everyone's birthdays. I guessed that if you four were all born within days of each other, then the others might be too.'

'Telling you about our powers might have been the best thing we ever did,' Parker responded, and everyone nodded in agreement.

Beau smiled at Tina, who grimaced.

'So, who is it?' Kyle asked eagerly.

'The people we should have suspected all along — Arlo and Devon Thomas.'

'I thought of them, but they were suspended during the school dance,' added Madison, 'and who would get close enough to them to create fusion; they're gross?'

'I thought the same, and the two girls born either side of

them seemed too random, but I changed my opinion today when I saw Devon making out with Mel.'

'Mel?' asked Parker, shocked.

'I know, how gross was it seeing her with Devon? You couldn't pay me enough,' responded Madison, missing the point of Parker's question.

'They were born May 12, and she's May 13.'

Suddenly, they could all see it.

Parker shuddered — taking on the Thomas twins terrified her.

'Hang on, I know who was born on May 11. Amie!' Madison was horrified.

Beau nodded, and Madison began to work it out in her head. The scary thing was, it all made sense. Amie had seemed distant, and she was often fond of borrowing money. She hadn't done it in weeks, yet she had been wearing new clothes.

'You mean Beau's Amy?' asked Griffin; the two Amys always confused him.

'No, Amie French, the one who I'm about to punch right in the face. It's one thing if your friend turns on you, Parker, but when one of my friends ditches me for the school trailer trash, that means war.'

Parker was used to Madison's bluntness; she'd even started finding it endearing.

The group discussed the possibility of their former friends teaming up with the awful Thomas twins. At first, they didn't want to believe it, but the evidence started piling up, and soon they were all in agreement.

'So now we know who, we need to decide what to do to stop them,' stated Tina, beating Beau to the punch.

He was not happy.

Just as Beau was about to lay out his quickly cobbled plan, the door to the room opened. Tina was ready to pounce on whichever student was about to enter.

However, it was not a student, it was a good-looking man dressed in a police uniform: Jeremy.

Everyone turned to face him, everyone quickly trying to hide their guilt. They hadn't seen Jeremy in days and were hoping he was gone.

'Here you are again, together. Some new faces as well. Are you seriously going to deny that nothing's going on in here?' Jeremy was tired of the run around he'd been getting from this group.

'These are all my students. I have them for English next. I was giving them assignment advice before class,' Tina responded. She was happy to see Jeremy; she just wished it could be socially.

'And my parents told you not to talk to me, maybe I should call them?' added Madison, her petulant side returning.

'Please, call them. Because our forensics team was around your house today. And what do you know? The scorch marks on your brother's walls match every other mysterious scorch mark we've investigated over the past few weeks.' Jeremy had them this time, and he knew it. 'So, what's going on kids? You can't deny that you're not involved anymore. I will get to the bottom of this, and you won't stop me this time.' He looked around the room and revelled in the panic he witnessed building on their faces.

CHAPTER TWENTY-NINE: PARKER vs ARLO

Jeremy seemed determined to discover the truth; however, he had underestimated a teenager's ability to hide the truth. He was sure they couldn't deny it any longer, but he was wrong, and Madison was happy to keep taunting him. She started to phone her parents, but Jeremy hurriedly left, promising this was not the end.

They didn't have time to worry about Jeremy for now. They needed to somehow stop Arlo, Devon, Mel and Amie. They weren't quite sure yet how they would do it, but they knew they had to. The power that generated deep from within their souls had created so many amazing moments; it had just saved the life of Madison's beloved brother. They were starting to believe that their powers could almost do anything they wished for. And right now, they wished to stop the others and make them accountable for the fire at their school and the lives they had taken.

For a short time, Beau feared his plan would never work ...

Griffin sat outside Mel's house, waiting for her to leave. Kyle had stayed outside watching till 1am the previous night, but Mel had stayed at home. Griffin had his earphones in, listening to a horror film podcast and waiting patiently. He was lucky the house across the road from Mel was for sale, and he could sit on the front verandah, hidden by the garden and the dark.

However, it was getting late, and Griffin was starting to get bored. It looked like tonight would be another strike out. The lights inside Mel's house went off at 11pm; her parents going to bed. Within five minutes, Griffin saw the fly screen on Mel's window shake loose. Griffin could see Mel's legs, followed by the rest of her body. She jumped from the window, looked around and then scuttled off to meet her boyfriend.

Griffin, adrenaline coursing through his veins, started to follow Mel from a safe distance.

Mel looked over her shoulder occasionally as she walked, this more from habit than any safety precaution.

Griffin pressed send on his prewritten text. This was not his secret phone; they'd been abandoned. The message read:

Mel is on the move.

Griffin was shocked when he realised Mel was leading him to the park where they once set a tree alight. This was only a stone's throw from Madison's house, and Griffin stopped, hiding behind a car parked on the street. He messaged his friends to come and join him.

He then carefully moved closer to the park. He knew there was a heavy blanket of trees, and he let the darkness of the night be his shield. Griffin moved closer, trying to listen to the voices he could barely hear. He could also follow the dark-blue glow now emanating from the park. He gathered his courage and peered through the trees. He knew that if he were caught, a terrifying lightning bolt would travel directly at him. When he finally looked, he saw Arlo and Amie stood hugging as Mel and Devon made out in front of them. With no schoolyard eyes watching them, they proudly let their dark-blue glow show their affection. Griffin was awestruck.

By the time Parker managed to sneak out the backdoor, Kyle was waiting in the front yard for her. They could still hear her parents inside, laughing at late night television. Madison also had to be careful; her parents were still in celebration mode. They were in their lounge room, drinks still flowing, and her mother was drunkenly singing along to Madonna's *Immaculate Collection* that played loudly from their old school CD player. By the time Madison crawled past the lounges her parents were sitting on, the others were waiting out the front for her.

Parker smiled as she saw Madison; they were nervous but knew they could do anything if they were together.

'Okay, team, time for the showdown!' Beau proclaimed proudly.

They had told Beau he probably shouldn't come along, but he assured them he'd be fine. He knew they could protect him. Beau seemed overconfident in the powers of his friends; they, however, were not quite as sure.

The four friends walked towards the park, the dark night seeming to match their thoughts. They were nervous, they were scared, they were unsure if they were strong enough to stop the Thomas twins.

Tina suggested they should tell Senior Constable Hill about the twins and their girlfriends. If they were arrested, they wouldn't be able to hurt any more people. But Beau put a stop to that, much to Tina's protest. If the others were arrested, there were no guarantees that they wouldn't spill the beans about their powers. The group couldn't take that risk. Beau was sure if Mel was interrogated, she would crumble into a mess. They didn't need questions being asked about teens with the power to generate electricity. Parker and Madison left themselves open to scrutiny when they saved Lachlan, leaving evidence across his bedroom walls, and then there was the convenience store.

Everyone knew Beau was right, and that sent them all into a state of panic.

As they approached the park, they could see the dark-blue hue that hung in the air. They turned to look at each other, and Madison and Parker stepped closer, ready to touch hands if needed. They jumped slightly as Griffin stepped out, his fear matching their own.

'They're all in there, and they're planning to hit another ATM tonight.'

Carefully, the five snuck through the thick trees, staying as close together as they could. They heard voices as they got closer, and the dark-blue glow seemed to be almost touching them. Making sure they made no noises as they reached the edge of the tree line, they slowed to a creep. Now they could clearly hear what the four were discussing.

'We need a new challenge, as we've mastered ATMs. I want us to go for something big again,' stated Arlo. The adrenaline rush from the armoured truck hold-up and the school fire was too addictive; he needed to feel it again.

'Whenever we go for something bigger, people get hurt. I don't want us to cause anyone else's death.' Mel was feeling more at ease in the group, she just didn't know that the sound of her voice drove Arlo insane. 'And don't we have enough money?'

No one else really agreed with that — they thought you could never have enough money. Amie had plans to take a trip to New York to shop her proceeds of crime away, and as for the boys, they couldn't stop if they tried.

'I'll tell you what, no money on the next one and no body count, we just have fun,' responded Arlo. Amie and Devon were ready to object, but Arlo hadn't finished. He smiled; he had just thought of the best plan. 'We all enjoyed that last fire. We don't need to hurt anyone, we just need to make a list of everyone we don't like, and we burn down their houses. Destroy all their stuff. Now that would be fun!'

Devon and Amie loved it, Amie hugging Arlo tightly. She loved Arlo's devious mind and was already making a list in her head of all the people's houses she wanted to burn.

Devon touched his girlfriend's shoulder; he knew she may not like the idea. 'We promise we won't hurt anyone, and we'll only pick the houses of people we *really* don't like.'

Mel knew she couldn't say no to the boys, she'd learnt that only too well. She smiled uneasily, Parker watched, not sure why Mel would go through with such an evil plan.

'Baldy has to be top of the list,' Amie added, keen to get the list started.

'Of course he is, that look on his face when we blew up his car was tops. I want to get that Ms Power too. Did you hear the way she was speaking to me today? She needs to pay!' Arlo had many possibilities in his head; he just had to get them into order.

The five friends hidden in the trees were horrified. Not only were their opponents becoming pyromaniacs, they were about to target their confidant and friend. They knew they couldn't back down; they needed to stop them tonight.

Devon was eager to start and asked who their first mark would be.

Arlo smiled his wicked smile that always made Mel uneasy. 'We do the first one for Mel, cause this was her idea.'

Mel gulped — this wasn't her idea at all, but she knew there would be no point arguing with Arlo.

'We hit that Parker chick.'

'What?' exclaimed Mel. That was the last person she expected Arlo to say.

In the cover of the trees, Parker felt the tears building. She could also feel the support of her friends around her. Beau hugged Parker in the dark. She was so glad he was there for her. Kyle looked on at them through the dark, and for a moment he wished he didn't have his power, then he could have been the one to hold her.

Arlo continued, 'She's used you for all these years, pretended to be your friend. Then the second some new kid comes along, she drops you. Now she's got this new group of friends that you're not welcome in.'

Mel thought Arlo was making a valid point. She felt abandoned by Parker; she couldn't see that she was the one who was pulling away when she'd hooked up with Devon.

'Parker's rubbing her new popularity in your face. She's even made friends with that slag Madison.'

Madison was ready to jump out then and there and shoot a lightning bolt into the back of Arlo's head.

Amie then spat out, 'I'm so sick of her. She reckons she owns the school. I'm tired of living in her shadow. I vote we hit Madison's house after we do Parker's, see how Miss Popularity likes all her junk well done.' She was no longer going to live in Madison's shadow. She'd had a taste of Arlo's God complex, and it was going down smoother than she could ever have imagined.

Madison was now even angrier; if it wasn't for Beau steadying her with his hands, she may have blown their cover.

'Done! Tonight, we hit Parker, Madison, Baldy and Power; one for each of us. We make this a memorable night!' Arlo chuckled as he spoke. He was so happy with the new plan. While he loved getting money, and they'd return to that soon, his favourite use of his powers was when he was seeking revenge. He was going to send dark-blue lightning bolts into houses while people slept. He didn't care if they got out safe, he just wanted to see people suffer.

The four finalised their plan. They would head to Parker's house first. They'd finish with Baldy Baxter — he was the main course. They knew the fire brigade would be busy battling the three other fires, so Baldy's house would burn to the ground before a single fire hose had been aimed at it.

They were ready to head off, Devon with his arm placed firmly around his girlfriend. He knew she was not entirely impressed by the plan, but Arlo had spoken, and they had to follow his lead. That was the way it was.

The five hiding in the trees were preparing to launch their attack. They planned as much as they could. Beau suggested they wait until the four were leaving before they attempted to stop them. They needed to catch them off guard, to gain an advantage; Arlo's team had far more practice than they did.

The five were ready ...

Arlo and his team were walking past.

It would only be moments before the five others would pounce.

But the exiting four were walking closer to them than they could have expected.

The five friends were worried they were going to be seen, so they carefully edged backwards, trying hard not to step on anything that would make any noise.

Parker was so careful with her feet that she wasn't looking up. She took a step backwards and a tree branch whacked her in the back of the head, knocking her off her feet. She started to fall, and Kyle leaned forward to catch her. As soon as she landed in his arms, they both began to glow.

The light and the noise of the fall alerted Arlo and his

gang. He realised someone was watching them, so he grabbed Amie's hand and shot a small lightning bolt into the wooded area, setting a tree alight and only just missing Griffin's face.

Madison screamed for them to join hands.

Through the dark, Griffin reached forward and held her hand. He had stayed a step behind her all night, desperate to protect her if needed. The glow the pair emitted helped Parker and Kyle find their hands. The four connected, and a lightning bolt shot from their hands. It mirrored their fierce determination and headed straight for the joined hands of Arlo and Amie, knocking them to the grass; smoke was billowing from their now blackened hands.

Again, on the word of Madison, the five sprinted from the protection of the trees, Beau hiding behind Kyle.

For the first time, the opposing forces were facing each other.

There was genuine surprise when Arlo and his team saw the faces of the people who had just sent Arlo and Amie flying. Mel began to cry when she saw Parker and Beau; she was caught red-handed, and she was regretting everything she'd done in the past month.

'What do you freaks think you're doing?' asked Arlo, swearing savagely.

'We're here to stop you,' Madison bravely retorted. This was her moment, and she was going to shine.

'You lot are a pack of losers; do you seriously think you can stop us? We're Gods,' roared Arlo, thrilled that he may still get the chance to add to his body count tonight.

'We shot open those doors in the school hall, and we're going to stop you tonight.' Parker's bravado was also growing, even though she felt like jelly on the inside. 'Gods or not!'

Amie stared at Madison and wondered if Madison had heard what she'd said earlier. While she was happy to bitch behind Madison's back, she never wanted Madison to know how jealous she really was of her. Madison's steely gaze frightened her, and as soon as she stood, she hid behind Arlo.

'And what do you reckon you can do to stop us? You're weak as.' Devon laughed teasingly, Arlo joining in. 'What could a bimbo, a nerd, an emo, a loser and a gay kid do to stop us?'

The five underdogs knew it wasn't a question to be answered with words, it needed action. They moved into formation — all four placing their hands on top of each other.

But Arlo was ready to counterattack. Without words, he and his team all held hands in a line. Their dark-blue lightning bolt shot from their hands, just as Parker, Madison, Griffin and Kyle touched. Their royal-blue lightning bolt meeting the dark-blue bolt. The two bolts of lightning fought for prominence, and sparks flew. Small fires began to start around them, and the cool night air became red-hot.

Beau stood behind his friends, calling for them to try harder. 'You can do this, work together, believe you can stop them, and you will.'

Those words were easier said than done. As soon as one bolt gained momentum, the other bolt seemed to fight back and regain ground. Blue sweat began to drip from all eight, and no one knew how this would end. Trees around them started to burn blue, and the light from the park was brighter than any warm summer's day.

Parker was beginning to think this was hopeless. Arlo's will was strong, and his beam was slowly making ground on theirs. She knew the key to victory was to turn them against each other; she needed to get Mel to pull away. 'Mel, this isn't you,' called Parker.

'You shut up and leave her alone,' Devon bellowed and pressed harder, making their lightning bolt push forward even more. They were getting dangerously close to Parker and her frightened friends.

'People are dead, Mel. I know that isn't you. Don't let them make you hurt any more people. I know you, Mel, I've known you since Kindy. I know your conscience couldn't deal with that.' Parker became teary as she spoke — she believed every word.

Arlo and Devon became more determined, but their bolt was losing some ground.

Mel's heart was starting to pull away from the fight.

'I swear if you don't concentrate, Mel, I'll go after your parents. I'll make you suffer.' Arlo's words were fierce, but it was too late. His words were having the opposite effect ...

Mel began to weep, and the dark blue from her face began to drain. She was closing herself off from the twins and becoming resistant to their powers. She fought her hand free, feeling pain from the hard grip of Devon.

With only three people against four, their dark-blue lightning bolt was disappearing fast. Madison called for her friends to finish them off, and the four tried even harder.

Before long, Arlo's bolt disappeared entirely.

A loud explosion rang through the park and the fires began to rage. A large blue cloud hovered above the area, and the residents of the neighbourhood all poured outside, concerned that someone had set off a bomb.

When the smoke began to clear, they could see Arlo, Devon, Amie and Mel all lying on the ground. They were surrounded by a circle of blue flames that slowly began to die down.

At first there was joy that the five had won the battle, but then concern took over. Had they killed them?

They rushed forward, but before they could check for

pulses, the now blackened teens were slowly waking up, groaning in pain.

Relief swept through the friends — they'd won for now.

Arlo opened his eyes, looking at the carnage around him, and he rubbed his eyes in shock. 'Where the hell am I?' He saw his brother waking up; confusion was written across their faces.

Amie and Mel were also dazed. Mel even asked Parker what had happened.

Parker was too shocked to respond.

Amie tried to stand but fell. Her hand landed on Arlo's ...

And there was nothing. No bolt came from them, no dark-blue light radiated.

Madison and Parker smiled at each other; it was over.

'Why are you freaks looking at us like that?' asked Arlo as he helped his brother up. They seemed to have no memory of what had happened. They were all dirty, they were all covered in ash, but none of them seemed to be radiating any dark blue. The lightning bolt of Parker, Madison, Griffin and Kyle must have stripped the others of their powers.

It was then that Griffin spotted another figure in the park. It was Jeremy, dressed in casual clothes. He had known something was going to happen. While Griffin was following Mel, Jeremy had been tailing Madison. He'd hid across the other side of the park and watched the action take place before him; he had seen it all. He was speechless and confused.

Sirens could be heard in the distance. The Emergency department received dozens of phone calls, and the police, ambulances and the fire brigade were all hurtling towards the park. Someone even tried to call in the army.

It seemed that the friends may have stopped the Thomas twins, but they were about to be exposed big time.

CHAPTER THIRTY: MADISON & GRIFFIN

The news crews knew the roads to the high school very well by now. Four students were charged with various crimes and were major suspects in the murders of a teacher and their fellow students. Mrs Arndell had scheduled a press conference in the hope that reporters would stop barging into classrooms and hounding every student in and out of the school gates. Everyone wanted to know about the students arrested and why these teens had committed these heinous crimes.

Parker walked carefully through the school gates, trying to look like any other student. But she was recognised by a reporter, who yelled, 'fry pan girl', and then all the reporters ran over to her.

'Is it true you're a close friend of Mel Abbott?' asked one reporter.

'Why do you think she joined two known felons to rob ATMs?' asked another.

Mr Baxter saw the reporters swarm around Parker and hurried across to save her. Kyle and Beau tried to distract the reporters, but they were desperate for information from Parker. The reporters even yelled abuse at Mr Baxter. They had heard a student mutter the word, 'Baldy' as a cruel nickname, and so even they began taunting him with calls of 'Baldy' as he ushered Parker into the safety of the school gates. He offered his sincere apologises to Parker and Beau about their friend. They smiled their thanks to him and then left.

Last night, the five friends couldn't believe that Jeremy had run across to them and told them what to say to the police. In those few moments in the park, Jeremy understood what had happened. He realised that the Thomas twins and their friends were responsible for the crimes that plagued the neighbourhood. He saw the battle, and he knew why the teacher had been protecting her students. Beau pleaded with Jeremy not to reveal his friend's secret, but Jeremy had already decided not to. He knew that they would never be left alone if this power was revealed, so he agreed to keep their secret.

The police arrived, and Jeremy handled the situation. He said he'd been with Parker and Madison when they led him to the park where they heard that the Thomas twins were preparing for another ATM hit. They were playing with explosives, and when they were surprised by Jeremy, the explosion went off. The Thomas house was raided, and all the proceeds of their crimes were discovered. The girls also had their houses raided, and a large pile of cash and gifts were discovered. The forensics team found no trace of explosives in the park, but they found the identical scorch marks that they'd been studying, and knew they had their culprits.

Arlo, Devon, Amie and Mel all pleaded innocence and were shocked when they were confronted with the overwhelming evidence against them. They claimed they couldn't remember anything that happened, but this was dismissed and all four were charged.

The Bennetts and the O'Sullivans were horrified to receive another call from the police. They rushed down to the police station, ready to abuse their children for sneaking out, and ready to abuse Jeremy again for questioning them.

Madison's mum's speech was slightly slurred; she was still feeling intoxicated from the night's celebration drinks. But when they heard their children were being considered heroes for helping the police solve major crimes, they were less upset.

Griffin's dad and Kyle's grandmother stood proud. Both had worried for the boys, worried about them socially, but now these fears seemed unfounded. The boys seemed to have found themselves some great friends and were happy.

It had been a long night for all the friends, and even though they were offered the day off school, they wanted to see each other the next day.

However, the night was far from over.

Griffin arrived home with his father, helping him out of the car and into his wheelchair. 'I'm sorry I snuck out, Dad,' Griffin said as he wheeled his father inside the house.

'All forgiven, my boy. You did a good thing tonight.' Bruce beamed at his son.

'Would you be angry if I snuck out again tonight?' Griffin nervously asked.

'Why would you need to do that?' asked Bruce, half-suspecting the answer.

'I want to see Madison before I lose my nerve.'

Bruce smiled at his son; how could he say no? He wanted his son to be happy, so he let him go with the promise he'd be home within the hour. There were so many police officers cruising the streets that Bruce knew his son would be safe.

Griffin ran to Madison's house, worried that if he stopped, he'd change his mind. The lights were off when he arrived at her house, so he cautiously headed towards Madison's bedroom window. He was surprised when he saw

Madison waiting by her open window. She grinned widely at Griffin, and his butterflies almost made him turn and run.

'I thought you'd be back,' Madison whispered, not wanting to wake up her parents. Well, at least her father, as she knew her mother was passed out from all the champagne she'd drunk earlier in the evening.

'You never answered me the other day. I like you. I really like you, and I want to be with you.' Griffin had been through too much tonight to be anything but brutally honest. The words seemed to fall from his mouth, but as soon as they escaped, his nerves returned.

Madison just smiled back. She should have answered him that day. She should have said that she had told Grayson she never wanted to see him again. She should have told him that if she were honest, she'd liked him all along. But all she said was, 'I want to be with you too.'

Griffin thought he would pass out. He couldn't believe the most beautiful girl in the school wanted to be with him. He gently leaned forward — he had imagined kissing her so many times that it almost seemed unreal that it was about to happen.

Madison was slightly nervous too. She'd only ever kissed Grayson, and now she was eager to kiss Griffin.

As they kissed, softly at first, a blue light radiated through the backyard and into Madison's bedroom. Britney scurried away, trying to hide under Madison's bed, but was only able to fit her head underneath. It was the most beautiful moment.

Madison smiled at Griffin; her heart was singing. She suddenly heard her parent's door open, and her father call out. She quickly kissed him again and sent Griffin off.

Griffin then ran the whole way home, desperate to see his father and tell him this was the best night of his life.

The four friends felt stronger after stopping Arlo and his team. It seemed like they had absorbed their powers. They also realised very quickly that they could now control when they emitted the blue light. This meant they could hold hands and not expose their powers. And so, they shocked the other students with their new relationships the next day at school.

Conversations stopped and mouths dropped as Madison and Parker happily walked the halls talking. On either side of them were their new boyfriends. Parker held hands with Kyle, and the big shock for all was Griffin and Madison. Amy walked beside them, cheerfully talking, raving about what wonderful couples they were.

They passed a subdued Grayson in the hallway with his parents. He'd been summoned to the office, knowing he would either be suspended or expelled. He saw Madison, happier than she'd been in a long time, walking with Griffin. He was devastated. Madison hadn't even noticed him.

Beau quickly caught up with the group. When he'd arrived at school, Xavier had rushed across to talk to him. Xavier apologised for not seeing him earlier. He'd been worried when he heard Beau was injured. He also praised Beau for his strength and hoped they could catch up soon for a coffee. Beau, slightly confused by the ambiguity of the conversation, was delighted none the less.

Before he could tell a curious Parker about the conversation, Beau's phone rang. He cautiously answered the private number. He smiled when he heard the voice; it was who he was hoping for. He told the caller on the other end that he would be there to see them soon and hung up. He then turned to his friends, smiled and revealed, 'I've done it, I found out when and why this all started.'

Parker and Madison turned to each other; they were

frantically eager to finally find out exactly where their powers had come from and exactly where their powers would take them.

ABOUT THE AUTHOR

Wayne Tunks is an award-winning filmmaker, playwright, and screenwriter with a love of pop culture, coffee and Madonna. His web series, 'After Nightfall', has won awards worldwide and he has been writing and producing plays for over 20 years. He is a former storyliner for TV's, 'Neighbours' and as an actor has appeared in some things you'd recognise and some you've never heard of. His most recent short film, 'Overcaterers Anonymous', is currently screening in film festivals worldwide and he is also the breakfast announcer on 80s radio station, My88FM. In 2021, Wayne released his debut novel, 'Normal or Nothing Like It'.

CPSIA information can be obtained
at www.ICGtesting.com
Printed in the USA
BVHW040443290622
640734BV00024B/34